FOUR WOMEN FROM RAVENSBRÜCK:

5 STORIES FROM THE SHOA

Roberta Kalechofsky

ISBN: 978-0-916288-57-0

Acknowledgements:
Four Women from Ravensbrück, previously published in *Job Enters A Pain Clinic and Other Stories*, **Micah Publications, 2005; My Poor Prisoner,** *Pulpsmith,* **1980,** *Phoenix Rising*, **Micah Publications, 1982,** *K'tia, A Saviour of the Jewish People,* **2006; Father Woytzski Leads A Jewish Youth Group to the Holocaust Memorial in Oswiecim, Poland,"** *Phoenix Rising,* **Micah Publications, 1982,** *K'tia, A Saviour of the Jewish People*, **Micah Publications, 2006; The Enigmatic Power of the Letter "J",** *The Long Story,* **no.24, 2006.**

MICAH PUBLICATIONS
www.micahbooks.com

To Kal

As Always

Their ancient glittering eyes were gay

-Table of Contents-

~~~~~~~
#
~~~~~~~

Four Women From Ravensbrück

"...the erotic availability became a coin of incommensurate worth, in return for which the chance of biological survival could be won."
Anna Pawelczynska, *Values and Violence in Auschwitz*

In a woman's camp the smell of female blood is everywhere. There are not enough napkins, and often the guards deliberately withhold them. Women bleed helplessly. The smell of blood from the women and the smell of alcohol from the guards mingle. The guards drink all the time, from morning till night. They cannot do their work without alcohol. The SS always have extra rations in their canteens. The smell of the female blood makes their heads swim. They pant like dogs. The smell of their semen, trapped in their pants, mixes with the smell of the alcohol in their mouths. On warm days, the whole camp smells of female blood, of female interiors. It makes the guards more vicious. They stroll through the camp, truncheons clenched in their fists, their eyes bloodshot from alcohol, circling the women like sharks around a bleeding stump. When they execute political prisoners, they strip them naked. When they take the women to the gas chamber, they strip them naked. They make them stand naked in the yard through roll call while they walk up and down and examine them. The

women cannot stop the searching hands of the guards, they cannot stop the teasing truncheon between their legs. The guards make them dig trenches naked, march naked, exercise naked, defecate in front of them naked, urinate, bleed, naked. They cannot get enough of looking at the women's bodies and examining them. They do this in the name of health measures and discipline. They cannot get enough of looking at the women. Their bodies excite them until they lose control, and they despise the women for this. They make the menstruating girls squat in the yard, their legs apart, so that they can watch their blood flow. They watch and pant and sweat and experience silent ecstasy.

Sometimes a guard swoons on the ground and writhes. Sometimes he masturbates furiously. The other guards laugh. It is a test of will among them to see which of them will be overcome by the smell of the blood. The female odor weakens them, and they hate the women for that. The women are glad when they have lost enough body fat and their menstrual cycles disappear. Their bodies find refuge in extreme remedies. They are no longer attractive enough to be raped. Their uteruses dry up and become desiccated butterflies. They lose hair everywhere. The mound of Venus becomes prepubescent. They terrify young girls who first arrive. The vanity of the outside world still clings to the newcomers, while the other women appear shameless in their retrogression, their missing teeth, their lice-bitten skin, their breasts shrunken to pubescent pimples over pubescent rib cages, their bodies bleeding irrelevantly to their intentions.

Fonya said that the only good thing about starvation was that it dried up the menses. "I have no use for all this womb apparatus." Some women agreed. "Here we have

no use for it. To be a woman here is a curse. To have a baby is a curse." Others wept for children they would never have, as if they had had them and lost them. Yet they pleaded with Magda, "the Aryan," to sing romantic songs to them. She was tall, slender and blonde and had been imprisoned for miscegenation. Wild rumors attached themselves to her. The women believed she had led a glamorous life in the outside world, singing in cabarets. She denied this. "Mostly we were starving performers. No one I knew ever succeeded in anything." They ignored her pathos and preferred to believe that she had been famous on the evidence of her long legs, her amber eyes, a husky voice like Marlene Dietrich's. She had been a singer, she said, because she was unfit to be anything else. "No business skills." After the war, she made no pretense to a stage career, and became a fortune teller in an amusement park. Nevertheless, they wanted to hear her sing, they insisted upon a performance. She refused at first. She had no sense of will or purpose except not to suffer, and to sing was to suffer. Everyone knew that to remember the past was to suffer. "It is too sad to sing such songs," she said.

But Magda always gave in to those who pleaded with her, and on nights when it seemed safe, she sang in the barracks in a low voice, songs like "Begin the Beguine" and "Blue Moon." She was right. The women floated out onto rivers of memory and wept.

Ravensbrück was built to house ten thousand prisoners. One hundred and twenty-three thousand women passed through it. After the war, many had been accounted for, who had survived, who had died and how. But Magda, Resi, Katerina and Fonya disappeared from the records.

The four women had been put on a truck one evening in February, 1943 for Dachau, and were not heard of again. Theirs was not a normal deportation. Such trucks never left the camp with only four women in them because it wasn't worth the gas. The camp was owned by Himmler and run for profit, as were the other slave camps, usefully set up on uncultivated wasteland that was good for nothing except to wring dividends from the lives of the slaves. The slave camps were Himmler's property. Shares in them were sold to shareholders, and revenue was collected from them by him. Extermination was not the object in Ravensbrück until August, 1944 when it was no longer profitable for the camp to keep its slaves.

The real object in Ravensbrück was profit, worked out in the ratio of the cost of a slave to her labor, to keep her alive as long as possible on as little as possible, and then to liquidate her as cheaply as possible, chiefly through the principle of extermination through labor: Arbeit Macht Frei. The profit motive drove everything: what the slaves ate, what they wore, how they died. Often slaves who were going to be killed were made to stand naked in the cold to weaken them further, so that less gas would be needed to kill them. Formal executions reserved for political prisoners took place within the enclosure where the cremation oven was located, which eliminated the need to transport their bodies. Nothing was wasted, not even disease and death which were administered with precision: how much the sick ate, who should be treated for illness, who would be given an extra blanket, the work schedules of the healthy slaves to the fifty-five factories that surrounded the camp, its four roll calls, its laundry room, its execution places, its transport system, its kitchen, its infirmary, its gas chamber, its cremation room, its morgue, its rankings of political prisoners, social outcasts, criminal prisoners, its modes of execution and identification.

The slaves were color coded. Each prisoner wore a triangle and a number sewn on the left sleeve of her striped jacket. Political prisoners like Katerina wore red triangles. Common criminals wore green triangles. Race defilers like Magda wore triangles with black borders around them. Jews wore two yellow triangles. Homosexuals wore pink triangles. Jehovah Witnesses wore violet triangles, Gypsies brown triangles. All others wore yellow triangles. Some categories overlapped: Jewish women like Fonya who had belonged to the French Resistance wore a red triangle on a yellow triangle; or prostitutes like Resi who had spied for the German Resistance wore a red and a green triangle. The sick and the elderly were sent to the infirmary to be poisoned. Other slaves were sent to the death camps to fill quotas there. The deportation trucks always took exactly a hundred and fifty women. Administrators, professors, doctors, nurses, truck drivers, secretaries, record keepers, bill collectors, came and went on schedule. Ravensbrück was a slave thanacropolis within walking distance of a Berlin suburb. In the spring, bicycle racers circled past the walls out into the countryside; young men and women picnicked not far away. When the sun shone on them, it shone on the slaves inside the wall; when the rain spoiled their picnic the slaves shivered in the downpour during roll call. When the slaves were sent to a work detail, those who got sick or slackened along the way were killed immediately, a blow to the head with a shovel or a bullet in the neck, while the other slaves stepped over their bodies.

No one registered reaction which could slacken their own steps, and then they too would be struck with the shovel.

Most often death came to the women through attrition, as they slipped from level to lower level until they broke through the biological net. You could see dead slaves standing upright, leaning against a building or on a shovel. These deaths were ascribed to natural causes. When a woman died from a beating, she may have first been raped, then starved, then denied treatment for typhus, made to stand naked in the snow or the hot sun, made to work in a factory while suffering from dysentery, perhaps made to watch her new-born infant drowned in a bucket of water. Typhus, gangrene, starvation, grief and exposure had exhausted her before the final blow from a truncheon brought her to the ground. The slaves lived in constant anticipation of death and died of dread at any provocation, a change in routine, a rumor or a glance. Sometimes they fell to the ground dead when their names were called, though no one had touched them. They collapsed and died when made to witness the strangulation of a child. They passed from weeks of grim stoicism to abject terror because of a guard's shout. The will to live disappeared if one's ration of soup was reduced.

Two symptoms revealed that a woman was coming to her end: the lice took control of her body and fantasy took control of her mind. Rumors overwhelmed her, and at Ravensbrück rumors ate the mind as greedily as lice ate the body. Soon one believed everything and could not distinguish anything. The mind darted from rumor to rumor, from lie to lie, from truth to lie. Then a single image of a food, a special cake or candy that had been a childhood holiday treat, hooked into the slave's brain and she would monotonously describe it in loving detail, saliva running over her lips, until the other women could stand it no more and were glad when she died.

The laundry room was the place where everything was sorted out, who had died, when, where and how, for their clothing was recycled to be de-loused and re-issued to new incoming slaves. The gold fillings and hair of those taken away came back to be reprocessed, the clothes came back to be laundered and used again. When women were deported to the death camps, their clothes often came back with messages stuffed into a pocket, a piece of paper with the owner's name and place of execution so that her friends at Ravensbrück would know where she had met her end. The laundry room was the center of information. Here Magda worked and saved whatever messages came her way, hiding them ingeniously. For what reason she did not know. Neither her name, nor the names of Resi, Katerina and Fonya ever came back, no message from them ever appeared, their clothes never returned. It was assumed that they had been executed in Dachau, and that their execution had been covered up for some reason.

The truck that came for them was not the usual van which took the slaves away to death camps. The typical February Berlin weather brought cold winds and sporadic hail. An abusive rain fell. The four women were ordered from their bunks in the early night. Each came from a different block and they did not know each other well. No common pattern united them except an idea in the head of SS Doktor Karl Rascher about hypothermia and body heat, an experiment he called "Project Lazarus," a wittily deceptive term like other Nazi code language. It was the idea of resuscitation through sexual stimulation, an idea which might occur to anyone who has been impressed with the power of lust to overwhelm other biological processes, except hunger. He had once arranged for an entertainment of mating bisons at Karin Hall at a party given by Goering. The building shook with the male animal's heat and the applause of the guests as the bisons reached climax. In the Kingdom Without Limits, one could join the primordial with the scientific, myth with rationalism, the instinct for life with the technology of death. Nature withheld nothing from the men with the truncheons.

In the morning no one spoke about the four missing women. Unexplained absences were pressure points the other women dared not push, fears about the brothel or the clinic. It was known that Professor Gebhardt had a clinic nearby for experiments in bone grafting and mustard gas and that there were "rabbits" at the camp, women who were sent there to be experimented on. Over a thousand women had been sterilized in the "infirmary" by Roentgen rays, had had parts of their reproductive organs removed and sent to the Research Institute in Breslau, had had silver nitrate poured into their oviducts, had had parts of their bodies, hips, shoulder blades, their blood and portions of their muscles taken from them for organ transplants into German soldiers. The bodies of dwarfs and cripples had been immersed in calcium chloride to preserve them and had been sent to research institutes for examination. Trucks crisscrossed Germany carrying bodies, organs, human flesh, stumps, skulls, limbs and female body parts. I.G. Farben had bought eighteen hundred slaves to test drugs. Many of the women preferred to be executed than to go there.

It eventually became known, in the way of concentration camp gossip, that Katerina, Resi, Magda and Fonya had been taken to Dachau, which could mean either the brothel or the clinic, for Dachau had both, and the better looking women were taken from Ravensbrück to service the brothel there: a term of six months and two thousand men. Resi joked that she preferred the brothel to the clinic on grounds of experience. She said she had worked in Kitty's in Berlin, though that was only temporary. The prostitutes there were never arrested, for the German generals went there, and Resi had the manners of the streetwalker, beaten and tough. There was nothing tempered about her. She could not survive without brashness, a brashness topped by tufts of red hair that remained after her head had been shaven. She had a hard time keeping her mouth shut until she was whipped twenty-five lashes for it, which left her subdued for two months.

Fonya's head was shaven too and was now covered with a black fuzz. She had joined the Communist Party, but left Russia when Stalin and Hitler signed their pact. Then she went to France and became a messenger for the group known as "Noah's Ark" in the French Resistance. For twenty years she had been on the move to find a political sphere for her restless body, her unappeasable loathing of corruption, tyranny, and cheating men. She had made a haphazard living writing articles, but they were too intemperate for most journals to find her work acceptable. Eventually everything disgusted her. She was a utopianist and could belong to no group for more than a few years, for as long as it took to reveal its hypocrisies and rivalries. Betrayal was ontological in her world. The other communists at Ravensbrück shunned her as an apostate. She didn't care. Contempt for human beings gave her an odd liberty. She maintained a resolute discipline in the camp: that she would do nothing that would help the enemy.

Katerina wore a crown of braids when she first arrived. She had come of the Russian aristocracy that had fled the revolution. She was her parents' only child, rooted in their exilic world, her nature shaped by their history, her intelligence formed by Russian tutors who were indifferent to altering circumstances of poverty and relocation. She spoke six languages and translated Tolstoy into German and Goethe into Russian and helped her father publish a newspaper for other Russian aristocrats living in exile. Some of the women called her "the snow princess," and endowed her with vestigial powers to "survive anything." They disliked her and respected her. She was not unkind, but she was armored, having decided that human evil was always incipient and its provoking moment was irrelevant. What mattered was a code of life that transcended human proclivities. Her family lived in a Russian world of Russian friends, Russian restaurants, Russian books and Russian music, confident that they would return to Russia when Europe returned to its senses. Her father had acquired a scar of honor from his left earlobe to the top of his neck in a duel with a German socialist. When he protested Hitler's pact with Russia, he was arrested and their paper was ordered shut, but Katerina continued to publish it underground until she was also arrested. After the war she went back to publishing the paper and waiting to return to Russia.

The night they were put on the truck for Dachau was cold, wet and sleety. An icy precipitation that was neither rain nor snow fell. Each drop of wet struck the ground like a missile. The four women were put into the back of a covered army truck which had been made comfortable for them and therefore aroused their suspicion: their status had been elevated to that of privileged prisoners. There were mattresses on the floor, thermoses of hot coffee, warm blankets and cigarettes. Resi clicked her teeth, "All the comforts of the barracks. Well, what do you think, ladies? When men get generous, what do you think they want?" The others shriveled under her words, but Resi stretched out on a mattress and said, "What the hell. I've been paid in worse coin."

Katerina retreated into a corner of the truck, clearing a decontaminated space around herself, and said in a voice futile in its authority, "They cannot mean to rape us here."

"Why?" Resi snickered, "are you particular about where the enemy fucks you?"

Magda said, "Let's not talk about what we do not know."

"Bullshit," Resi, said, "we know." Her clarity rebuked them and they stopped talking. The icy rain hit the canvas covering over the truck and drew attention to the cold outside. The truck lurched forward into gear and was soon traveling at high speed. They paid attention to everything the truck did, when it stopped, when it seemed to turn, when it slowed down, when it picked up speed again, though their knowledge would not make any difference. They did not know they were going to Dachau. They did not know where they were going or why and preferred not think about it. They preferred, at first, to sit suspended without thought or speech until their silence began to suffocate them more than their fears. They were powerless to stop the truck. They could only suffer thoughts until they would know why they had been removed from Ravensbrück and then suffer reality. One could die of their thoughts.

The trip took ten hours and time moved slowly. Every so often someone stirred, lit a cigarette, stretched a leg. The muffled movement made the silence more apparent and encased them in isolation from each other. From time to time the truck slowed down, perhaps waited for a light. They heard the noise of the huge windshield wipers. Then the truck started again to their relief. Anything was better than arriving. There was a hair's width of space between the canvas covering and the truck. An occasional beam of light from an opposite car on the road swung into the opening like a knife's blade, the sound of its motor sadly delicious until it disappeared into the rain, and they sat again in silence, suspended inside the machine.

"It's better to talk," Resi finally said resolutely, and lit a cigarette.

Magda agreed. "But not about now."

"What then?" Resi asked. She passed cigarettes and matches around. Fonya and Magda accepted. Magda shivered, though they had been given coats to wear over their striped shirts. Resi pushed a blanket at her. "Might as well have it," she said. "They will never be this generous again."

"I will take some coffee," Fonya said, and reached for a thermos.

Katerina took some too and said, to dispel the poisonous silence and make a pointed comment such as visitors or tourists might make, "What an awful climate Berlin has in the winter. In Russia at least cold weather is beautiful."

"You miss Russia?" Magda said with curious sympathy. Katerina did not respond, but Fonya said to her, "Why should you? You've been here more than twenty years. I don't miss Russia. I don't miss anything or any place."

"Neither do I," Resi said. "The past is a bummer. Besides, how can you remember what the weather was like in Russia if you were three years old when you left? My parents died when I was three, both in the same week of the flu. I can hardly remember them. I'll bet you don't remember Russia at all. You only think you do."

Katerina did not care to discuss how memories persist and Resi said, "I had a picture of my parents that I kept for years, but when I left my uncle's house he took it from me, and now I can't remember what they looked like."

"I remember everything," Fonya said, "but I didn't leave Russia until I was twenty-two. If you stay in a place until you are grown it's easier to remember it."

"But you don't miss Russia?" Magda asked.

"No. I don't miss anywhere," Fonya said again.

"Did you grow up in Berlin?" Magda asked Resi, determined to keep the talk going.

"No, in Lübeck. That's where I come from. I ran away to Berlin to become an actress. Every prostitute thinks she's going to be an actress."

"Why did you become a prostitute?"

"No special reason. After my parents died, I was sent to live with an uncle. I hated him and he hated me. He never let me do anything. He hated the music I listened to, he hated American jazz, he hated the way I dressed, he hated everything I did, he hated the way I talked and walked. So I ran away to Berlin. Six months later I was starving and a pimp set me up. He said I would never go hungry again if I stuck with him, and he was right about that. There's permanent occupation in sex until you grow old. Frankly, I don't care where they fuck me, as long as I get fed. I've been fucked so often, I know how to shut my eyes and disappear. I've been a prostitute since I was fifteen and now I'm thirty. I averaged two men a night, seven nights a week, for fifteen years. The number comes to 10, 080."

"Good for you," Fonya said."

"Oh, God," Katerina said.

Resi acknowledged both tributes. "The number surprised me too when I added it up. But I think my experience has saved me so far. I'm sure the Gestapo would have killed me by now if they didn't think they could fuck me some more."

"I was an actress," Magda said. "You can also starve as an actress."

"Tell us," Resi said. "I like to hear about any life that was more successful than mine."

"You'll have to get someone else to give that story. I was a very bad actress. Actually I never got on to a real stage. Mostly I did song and dance routines in cabarets. My boyfriend wrote the songs and I sang them. We starved together." She laughed uncomfortably, aware of disturbing their illusions. "He was very talented, but I was an ordinary singer. His songs needed someone with dramatic flair, like Lotte Lenya. Mostly it was my fault that we starved, but he wouldn't leave me."

"Well, obviously, I was not a successful actress either," Resi said, "but I was a successful whore. After fourteen years on the street I managed to get myself a job at Kitty's. One of their girls succumbed to a disease just when they were giving a big party for German generals. They were desperate and picked me up, cleaned me up and dressed me up. I realized one can actually have a good life as a whore."

"Then you were successful once," Magda said. " I worked for the worst nightclubs in Berlin. Maybe our patrons were not so different."

"Yes, they were different," Resi said. "The patrons who came to Kitty's were very high class, diplomats and generals."

"Why were you arrested then?" Katerina asked.

Resi declined to tell her that the underground railroad of information and rescue went through brothels and convents, from streetwalkers to partisans. She said instead, "I guess I just didn't like big pricks and the Gestapo found out. I've seen too many men naked in bed to take a uniform seriously. I'd been arrested before, many times. So what the hell, I thought, another night in jail and I'll be out. Why would I think anything else? What about you?" she asked Magda, "why were you arrested? You're so pure Aryan looking. You'd think they'd keep you as a prize."

"Yes, of course, but that's why they considered me a traitor. My lover was Jewish. Either I betrayed him or I betrayed them."

Katerina said, "At least you had a choice."

Fonya exploded. "You call that a choice! I'm from Russia too, the other Russia, the one that never had a choice. Besides, after Stalin came to power, what was the choice between him and the other one, between one evil or the other?"

Magda intervened. "It's always a choice between evils, don't you think? Werner and I had been childhood sweethearts, I can't remember for how long. He seems always to have been part of my life. He was very talented, wrote songs like Brecht, when he was sixteen he played three instruments in the jazz bands, piano, trumpet and drum. I loved his life more than my own. My father was a school teacher, my brothers joined the Brown Shirts. We quarreled constantly. My father wanted me to break off with Werner, so I ran away and joined his band. It was fun for a while, but we were always out of money. We were so poor that we were often hungry. Then they began to arrest our friends. Werner pleaded with me to leave him, but I wouldn't, and I pleaded with him to leave the country, but he would not go without me. My father had died and I could not leave my mother. Then my mother died a year later. Poor woman. It was terrible to think that we had waited for her to die so that we could leave the country. But as soon as I closed her eyes, I called Werner and said, 'We're free. Nothing holds me here anymore.' But it was too late. They had found out about us. We also thought it was ridiculous, that the regime would not last. We gave peroxide parties. Everyone bleached their hair. The whole band, even the Negroes from America. We gave out bottles of peroxide to our audience. People bleached their hair then and there in the cabarets. We had wonderful parties, which is strange to think about now, because we were always hungry and frightened. We played all the American songs and danced until dawn. Werner and I loved to do the tango and the two-step. Slow dancing, any kind of slow dancing. He was a wonderful dancer."

"I would rather dance than fuck," Resi said.

"Me too," Fonya said, "especially if it's slow dancing. Once I had a boyfriend in Paris who danced very well. He was impotent, but what a dancer."

"I should have such luck," Resi said.

"No," Magda said, "You should not. The truth is we danced until total exhaustion so that we wouldn't have to face our empty cupboards. We thought it was fun because we were all together, everyone gripping someone around the waist, sleeping on our feet, moving around and around until dawn, the whole cabaret swaying."

"It sounds like fun to me," Resi said. Magda did not respond to this, and Resi amended her judgment: "I guess it wasn't."

"No, it wasn't," Magda said, "it was desperation, but we called it fun."

"Where is Werner now?"

Magda stirred in the dark, a hardly discernible movement, like her talk, barely audible in the historical record. "He is gone. Everyone is gone. Little by little everyone's hair turned back to its original color, and more and more cabarets were shut down, more and more of our friends were arrested. I became depressed, and when you are depressed your thoughts are very strange. I don't know why I thought suicide was better than our parting, but so it seemed at the time. Many of our friends were committing suicide. We threw suicide parties. Perhaps if I had had more to eat, I would have had the strength to think of something better to do. I decided I would also throw a suicide party. Many of our friends were doing that. I bought bottles of champagne and wonderful cheeses and set a table in my apartment, with balloons and ribbons. I spent all the money I had. Then I called my friends to come to the party, I swallowed a bottle of pills, lay down on my sofa and pinned a note to my chest: 'Please do not revive me. And please make sure I am dead before you bury me. I do not wish to wake up in my coffin, underneath the earth, alone. I will wait for you, Werner, but do not hasten to join me. Let me hear the band play my favorite songs and I will dance away into the night. My eternal love, Magda.'

Well, when you are young, you sometimes do things like that." She laughed. "Yes, I wanted my friends to celebrate my death. I was tired of being cold and hungry. I was always shaking with fright, even before Mühsam's arrest, and Werner was always consoling me. 'It will not last.' I do not know where all my fear came from, and I was tired of it. I seemed to have been born frightened. But Werner revived me. He lay down on top of me and wept. I smelled his hair, his breath, his grief, and I returned. Everyone thought it was a good joke. We had a wonderful party. Then one night when Werner walked me home from the cabaret, he told me I must go, I must leave Germany. He did not think he would be able to get out anymore. I must go myself, he said. I tore at him, 'Then why didn't you let me die. You know I can't bear to be lonely. I don't know how to live by myself.' It was bitterly cold. I had barely a decent coat on me. We spent maybe five minutes together and quarreled. It was so dangerous for us to be on the street together. 'Listen, Magda,' he said, 'I will not have you staying on my account. Go away, you must go away while you still can. This won't last and eventually I will find you.' I shook with fear, maybe from the cold, I don't know. I could barely talk. 'I'm not the one in danger,' I said.

'Yes, you are,' he said, 'you are in danger because of me. We must stop seeing each other.' I could not bear to hear him say this. I began to scream and two SS appeared immediately on the street. Werner ran off and melted away into the dark. The guards asked me what was the matter. I said I had been seized with a stomach cramp. They called a taxi for me and it drove me home. From a shadow on the street, I saw Werner running away. That was the last I saw of him, darting between the buildings. I was afraid to roll down my window and call to him. All night I imagined that the guards had shot him in the street while he was running. When my phone rang six o'clock in the morning it was his roommate. I thought he was calling to tell me that Werner had not come home last night. I knew he was gone. I knew it in every part of my body. 'Come quick,' Gunther said.

'Where is Werner?' I asked.

He paused for a second. 'He is here.' He's lying, I thought, as I ran down the steps. But why would he lie? What would be the use of it? Werner must be there, after all. I arrived fifteen minutes later. Gunther opened the door. He was pale and disheveled. He took my hand. 'Be brave,' he said. 'You lied,' I screamed. 'You said Werner was here.'

'He is here,' he said and pushed open the door to the bedroom. Werner lay on the floor, his head swimming in blood, a gun in one hand, a note in the other. It said, 'Magda, my love, go.'"

Her voice changed. It affected a silly irony. "My suicide note was more interesting, don't you think? And anyway I had nowhere to go. I am as content to be here as anywhere else."

Katerina said, "That is defeatist. One must not think that way."

"Yes?" Magda said.

"Yekaterina," Fonya said warily, "You want to know why I became a communist? To save me from people like you. I ran away from home too, I ran away to become a communist, a free woman, so that people like you could not step on people like me."

Katerina considered this statement. "And did you succeed?" she asked.

"At least I tried to put my destiny into my own hands, not into my father's."

"You women are so fucked up," Resi said. "I wish I had had a father who cared about my destiny."

"No, you wouldn't," Fonya said, "if you had had a father like mine who cared more about your virginity than about you."

"Why shouldn't he care about that?" Katerina asked. Resi shrugged her shoulders at both of them. "It's tough to be fifteen."

Fonya agreed: "It's too bad we have bodies before we have wisdom."

"That's why we have fathers," Katerina said.

Magda asked Fonya, "Were you raped?"

Fonya thought about this for a moment. "Yes," she said, "in a manner of speaking."

"No one is raped in a manner of speaking," Resi said.

"It was worse than rape," Fonya said, "I was raped in my soul. My father didn't like anything I liked anymore than your uncle did. We lived in a small town. My father was the baker there. Everyone bought bread from him, even the Gentiles. He was the only baker in the town, and I used to help him. There was a boy, a Gentile, who used to come every Thursday to buy bread from us. His mother was bedridden and he did the shopping for her. He was so handsome, with blonde hair and blue eyes, a real shaygitz, my father called him. Every time he came into the store my body turned to water. I was about fourteen and he was probably sixteen. When he came into the store and looked at me with his blue eyes I felt flames shoot through my thighs. I could hardly stand on my feet or touch his hand when I gave him the bread and took the money. Week after week he came every Thursday morning. I was a nervous wreck waiting for him. If he touched my fingers, they shot into flames, if he touched my arm it burned the whole afternoon."

Fonya was astonished at how vivid the memory still was, though she would have like to cut it out with pincers. Still, she succumbed to the memory: "All week I could think of nothing but seeing him on Thursday. I lived for the few minutes he came into the store and if a week went by and he did not come that Thursday, I got sick. I couldn't eat. I ran a fever. What an incurable disease! When he came into the store, sometimes I thought his eyes rested on my face longer than necessary, and I felt my cheeks burn. Sometimes I thought his eyes looked directly into mine and tried to send me a message. I imagined all kinds of things. I imagined he was lonely and longed for me. I imagined he stood by his window as I stood by mine and watched the street to see when I passed, as I watched the street for him. I imagined I was being unkind to him because I never smiled at him when I saw him in the store. I was too frightened to smile because of my father. I imagined that he knew it would be dangerous for me to smile at him and that he was thinking of a safe way to contact me. One day I went to visit a friend in the next town and was coming home through the meadow. It was spring. My breasts were so heavy, they ached. The sky was filled with birds and the earth smelled of clover and buds. My body was filled with longing, even before I saw him. He was crossing the meadow too, almost directly in my path. My legs turned to stone. I could not move them. I could not move from the spot. I saw that he changed his direction so that his path would cross mine. Immediately I thought that this must be the plan he had thought of to see me, that he walked here every afternoon hoping to meet me here. Where else could we meet? Why else would he be here now? I felt terrible that I had not thought of this before, that I had kept him waiting. I felt remorse that I had been stupid, that I had caused him pain." She laughed ruefully, "Can you believe that? Innocence is terrible. As he approached me I thought I saw in his eyes desire and acknowledgement. He smiled at me with such a wonderful smile. I could not stand on my legs anymore now that he was so close to me, his eyes against mine, his legs against mine. We fell to the ground together. The grass covered us. Flocks of birds flew across the sky like a banner. 'Do you love me?' I whispered. 'What?' he said. I sank into the earth. When he was done, he buttoned up his pants and continued on his way. I lay there for hours. My father and my brothers came looking for me and when they found me

they asked me if I had been raped. I said I had become dizzy and had lain down to rest. I should have lied and said I had been raped. It would have been better for me. I had been raped, I had been raped in my soul. My father was suspicious, but said nothing. But now he watched me all the time. Every day became a burden. He would not let me out of the house, I could not even help in the store anymore, which was just as well. He said I was a woman with naked eyes and that he would find me a husband to cover them up. When I missed my period for two months I became terrified and ran away to Moscow and found some Jewish girls there who helped me deliver my baby."

The truck stopped momentarily. Everyone became alert. The rain fell, each drop hard as a stone on the canvas. They expected any moment to see the searchlights swing into their faces, to hear the guards shout at them, "Mach schnell, mach schnell." But the truck started again, and they were relieved.

"I have nothing more to be afraid of," Resi said.

"Me too," Magda said. "It is odd that I am no longer afraid."

"What became of your baby?" Resi asked.

Fonya's voice lowered to a confessional tone. " She was a girl with blonde hair. I gave her away for adoption to a Gentile couple." Then her voice hit its customary stride. "It has always seemed strange to me that a woman can bear the child of a man she has scarcely known. Nature cares nothing about us. Nature is our enemy. It was all for nothing."

Resi laughed. "I wouldn't say that. At least you had a five minute illusion. I never even had that much."

"Five minutes!" Fonya spit. "One can also say at least you never had any illusions, which is better. I was raped in my soul, and I should have told my father that I had been raped, because that was the truth."

"You never had other lovers?" Magda asked.

Fonya replied derisively, "Yes, of course. I had other lovers, I had other lovers all the time, if you wish to call them lovers. I could never get rid of the need for sex, but love, please!" She clicked her teeth with disgust. "Listen, Resi, a woman can live without love, but some women like me cannot live without sex. Nature is our worst enemy. I have no use for men but I cannot change myself."

"You've never had a lover?" Resi asked Katerina, boldly.

Katerina answered equally boldly, "My parents have selected a husband for me and I do not allow my mind to wander."

"And you've never seen him?" Magda asked.

"Pictures," Katerina said.

Resi digested this for a while. Then she asked, "How do you know you will like him?"

"How many of the 10, 080 men you've slept with have you liked?"

"None."

"Sex is over-rated," Fonya said, "but apparently inescapable, like an avalanche. So why am I required to equate it with my eternal soul?"

"People write songs about love," Magda said. "They don't write songs about avalanches, unless you lose your lover in one."

"It's ridiculous," Fonya said. "Either he has egg on his beard, or his breath smells of vodka and cigarette smoke. Half the time I get a headache."

"Or he doesn't have an orgasm and wants his money back," Resi said. "Dancing is better."

"True," Magda said, "especially the tango. Especially the wonderful tango, When Orchids Bloom in the Moonlight," and she began to sing. "It's true," Resi said. Fonya said, "It's all a dream. It's either a dream or a nightmare."

The truck stopped again and Magda stopped singing. Then the truck started again, but slowly. They surmised they were no longer on the highway, most likely on a side road. Perhaps they were arriving. Yes, they were arriving. The truck rolled to a stop at a gate, questions were asked, identification papers were passed. A soldier unpinned the canvas to the truck and ordered them out. "Mach schnell, mach schnell." They climbed out of the truck. The gates of Dachau rose out of the morning fog. The sight was familiar, the slogan over the gateway was familiar, the architecture was familiar, utilitarian, dismal, barren. The fog shrouded the slaves in the camp in their striped pajamas. Their gaunt forms rose like spectres from the mists as they pulled tractors and trucks and shoveled snow. A western wind carried the smell of burning flesh.

The four women were rushed into the administration building, registered, paid for, and taken to the hospital. Their nerves unravelled utterly at the sight of its white functional concrete walls. They were pushed into a shower to be deloused with shouts again of "Mach schnell, mach schnell," and taken to a room with beds, a table and chairs. Clothes and food were brought to them. Nothing was clarified. No one explained anything to them. The sight of the food made them weep with a frightened hunger, but Katerina reminded them that the Nazis would not waste clean clothes on them if they intended to poison them. They gave into their hunger and ate the food meticulously, then waited for their destiny to unfold.

No one came to explain it for several hours, and the silence became omnivorous again, eating into their brains. Resi tried to joke: "I hope it's a brothel." No one responded. They could not make the effort at conversation again. The room was warm and they perspired. Their bodies melted in the silence. Outside, slaves went by in the fog carrying bricks in a wheelbarrow. In the distance other slaves marched to a factory. A patch of cold sun emerged and lit up the heads of two slaves who had been hanging from poles for several days, probably not yet dead, or not dead enough. Only the circling birds would know.

At last, the door opened and Dr. Rascher in pressed military uniform and another doctor in a laboratory coat entered. They looked as if they were in opposition to each other, the military man and the medical man, rather than accomplices as they were. Dr. Rascher surveyed the four women for a few seconds. They had an impulse to move together, to cover their bodies, but dared not move. For his part, he was pleased at the combination of women he had acquired. He had hoped to carry out his hypothermia experiments at Auschwitz on a grand scale, but had had to settle for the acres of cold foggy fields and a few tanks of icy water at Dachau. Nevertheless, he had adequate means. Dachau was situated within sight of the Alps. Winters were severe here. Snow often fell from the end of November through April. If the natural climate could not freeze a naked man by prolonged exposure, his temperature could be lowered by submersion in icy water.

The women knew nothing of his ambitions and when he finally spoke, his speech nonplussed them. He told them that, as a Nazi officer, he had great reverence for women; he explained the scientific usefulness of his experiments which were being conducted on behalf of the German Air Force; that everything was being done to assure the scientific quality of the work, measurements of the test person's body heat were taken every ten minutes; that the gain for humankind might be immeasurable; that they, as women, were being honored in their role to contribute to this undertaking.

The sweat crawled through their bodies like lice. They failed to grasp what was expected of them and felt more confused with every word he spoke. He hated to be unromantically explicit. Prudery and vulgarity combined in him in a new manner out of different limits. He decided they were being deliberately obtuse. There was an unsavory aspect to this part of the experiment which could not be clarified in advance: could he trust their compliance, their meaningful compliance? When you came down to it if you couldn't trust their compliance, the experiment was useless. There were many instances when men could dispense with women, except as a germinative thought. The German resurrection was, after all, a male event. Last night he woke in the flush of a spontaneous erection and his wife was asleep like a stone. But who was master of whose fate? He grasped his organ in his hand and moved it slowly, and then faster. But this was not one of those events. Compliance was required here. It should not be difficult for them to understand what was expected of them even though it was difficult for him to tell them what he expected them to do. The doctor by his side did not attempt to help him, for he was too prudish and preferred not to put into speech, beyond the confusing statement, 'embrace them and bring them back to life.' But in the Kingdom Without Limits, citizens can go from charm to hatred, from good manners to rage in the twinkling of an eye. It was Dr. Rascher's prudery that had confused them. As soon as he screamed at Resi, "You! Don't pretend ignorance!" they understood.

Still, as enlightenment crept across their faces he thought he detected craftiness in them and his rage increased. He screamed at Fonya, whose recollection of the passage was hazy, "You Jews thought you could save your king David this way with Abishag. Why should you be embarrassed?" He chuckled as he grasped his precedent; in fact, he grasped several precedents: "There is nothing new under the sun," he said with brutal emphasis in case anyone should blame him for this innovation, and turned and left. His assistant followed with relief. The door closed and the women sank onto their cots, while the cold sweat dried on their bodies.

Resi said after a while, "Jesus Christ, this must be the limit. I'm not going to screw a stiff. Who's Abishag anyway?"

Fonya told as much as she remembered of the story. "So, it is true," Resi said, "we really do have incredible powers."

"That seems to be our misfortune," Fonya said maliciously.

"But not enough to warm a stiff," Resi said.

"Don't use that language," Katerina screamed with disgust. "Anyway, they're not dead."

"They'll be close to dead," Magda said. They tried to understand this.

"How close?" Fonya asked. No one knew, or cared to say. Something imponderable was in the circumstances, something beyond the imagination of sex, romantic or obscene, something without a history to it.

Katerina covered her eyes with an arm. "I won't do it. I won't do it." Fate had outwitted her: a first embrace in an arctic region on a hospital floor under the gaze of instruments and doctors.

Fonya said wearily, "I can't kill someone if I think I can save him."

Katerina jumped up from her cot with rage, the blood drained from her face. "That is a stupid idea, to put life above everything else, above dignity and honor. Is that part of your Jewish communist training?"

Fonya screamed at her, "You're a fascist like the rest of them. The fact is you're a frozen virgin fascist and you're afraid even to give your precious virginity to save a dying man."

Magda cried, "What is the use of our fighting with each other? The fact is that if we succeed it would also help the Germans. Let's not forget that."

"My God," Resi said, aspiring to brazen reality, "if we succeed, they'll round up every prostitute for this work."

That crushed them into silence, a silence like a concrete wall they could not scale. It would always be there, the final end beyond which their thoughts could not go. Fonya hissed under her breath, "Under no circumstances will

I help the enemy. That's the last piece of honor I have left." Resi agreed: It was one thing to fuck for money, to save your life, to save a king; it was another thing to fuck to help the enemy to victory. "But they will kill us if they suspect us," she sneered, "of withholding our meaningful compliance."

"They'll probably kill us anyway," Fonya said, as if that was a consolation. "Let's not be tempted by an illusion, and let it not go into the record that they succeeded in this experiment because of us."

No one argued further after this. Their silence spoke for them. They were prepared, all except Katerina, to buy life with their bodies, but not to help the enemy. It was the one thing they all agreed on.

But they were not killed in Dachau. Death came to them in other ways. By a chicanery of circumstances they were deported from Dachau, each to other camps, finally liberated with "certificates of disappearance," and went their separate ways. When the information about the hypothermia experiments at Dachau came to light at the Nuremberg trials it was known that women had been brought to the men, that they had embraced frozen lovers, but as no useful data emerged from this aspect of the experiment little mention was made of it in subsequent references to these experiments, or of the women who had been brought there. After the war, Fonya went to the United States, where she moved from job to job and place to place, still restless, belonging nowhere, waitressing in San Francisco, doing housework in New York. Once she lived with a young man for a few weeks, until she woke one morning and saw an eye on her full of cold agony, and flesh that felt like fish in a barrel of ice, its gills barely palpitating.

Perhaps her lover had died. She could not tell. In very cold temperatures, signs of life become puzzling to interpret and it is difficult to know whether one is choosing life or death. One could embrace a dead man and not know it. Abishag's blessing had turned into a curse, but Fonya did not care. Ice is good. Disease cannot spread in ice. Her own body was finally dead. She was glad about this and took no more lovers.

Katerina went back to her small apartment to nurse her aging mother, and put the photograph of her intended husband away. She did not plan to marry. Resi went back to the streets, and each time she picked up a man she pretended she was Abishag being brought to King David to heal him, but she knew that the men she picked up had the anonymity of frozen flesh.

Magda had a one room apartment on the third floor of a walkup in a poor neighborhood and took refuge in small comforts: fresh flowers when she could afford them, an old velvet sofa which she used as a bed, a phonograph bought from a junk shop, old records saved from destruction: the Dorsey band, Harry James, Brecht, Benny Goodman. She still preferred the music from this era. The cabarets were opening again in Berlin, but the music was different, the entertainment was different. In the poorer neighborhoods on her route from the amusement park to her apartment, she passed caverns that showed underground movies with strange titles and live sex shows. Flesh was everywhere, promising everything, dissolution, violence and orgasm, an end to the dilemmas of the body. Last week a dead prostitute had been found, her head here, her torso there. Organs and limbs and body parts had surfaced for days. Memories returned to her of women sitting in their menstrual blood, their bodies dissolving on the ground, and there was no antidote for this, no future to prevent the past from returning in memories or otherwise. All eyes looked dead to her, all flesh numb, all faces frozen in their expressions, unbearable to touch. Her old love, preserved like an ideal from youth against such betrayal, a flower pressed between granite, became more powerful to her than life itself. Only death could save this love from the betrayal she saw around her. One night, she put a tango on her phonograph, turned on the gas in her stove and laid down on her couch. This time she did not leave a note.

#

MY POOR PRISONER

For Erich Mühsam, 1878-1934

There is an unpleasant incident which took place in the fortress of Oranienberg in 1934, when the quixotic cabaret poet of the 1930s, Erich Mühsam, was brought there and imprisoned in the Gestapo roundup of left-wing intellectuals after the Reichstag fire.

Mühsam was known in Berlin circles as a "kaffeehaus poet," bohemian in style, outrageously satirical in his poetry, and Blakean too, as if his writing was squeezed out between bitterness and vision. He was physically unmistakeable: bushy red hair and a wild red beard crowding an emaciated face; scrawny body and wiry fingers. He was loved by his friends and hated by his enemies for the same quality: "something Christ-like," the friends said sentimentally and his enemies said snickeringly, when anecdotes were told of him, of how poverty-stricken Mühsam, who had scarcely seed to put in his mouth, gave his coat to a beggar. The comparison was subtly unflattering, and he snickered back with a manic need to bait, "Why not something Jew-like?"

Nor could he resist the visionary in him from working out a similar compulsion towards destructive acts of generosity, when some friends--for he had them not only among the bohemian writers of Berlin, but even a few randomly powerful ones--secured him a train ticket to Prague when it was known that the Gestapo was looking for him.

As luck would have it, a similar set of circumstances surrounded another young man, also wanted by the Gestapo, except that we know nothing more about him than this: as Mühsam had his foot on the first step of the train, he saw the conductor rough-handle this man who was trying to board without a ticket. The look on the man's face tore Mühsam's caution from him.

"It's all right," he said to the conductor with a disappearing smile. Anything more would have been superfluous, for when offered the ticket the young man grabbed it and ran, and Mühsam's singular generosity is recorded with the enigma embedded in his personality. He did his last act as a free man to the conductor and to a platform of strangers who indulged him with smiles.

"Quite all right," he said to them, for the young man had disappeared into the train, "please don't thank me. Think nothing of it. Well, hey! I've been in prison before. Put your consciences at rest. I can perform there as well as anywhere," and he blew them a kiss.

He was arrested the next morning. If the other young man had been imprisoned instead, if Mühsam had taken the train to Prague, if Jesus had not been crucified, the following thoughts about good and evil would not have been written for, aside from the fact that Mühsam felt an affinity between himself and Jesus, there are some events which suck the whole of an era into them. Beyond the heart-rending nature of the following episode--the torture of an animal to get at the poet (the sole aim of his jailers was to drive Mühsam to suicide) there is the fact of its parallel in the days of Nebuchadnezzar, and the difference in the two cultures: that when the lion refused to do the guards' bidding and attack Daniel, they did not revenge themselves upon the animal by torturing it, but took it as a sign from the Hebrew's God and let the Hebrew go.

Night after night, morning after morning, they tortured the chimpanzee and brought Mühsam to look at her, and whispered in his ear: "Why don't you kill yourself and save this poor animal her agony."

The chimpanzee lay shriveled in a corner. Much of her fur had been torn from her. Keeping her conscious, they had carefully mutilated her teats. Her skin was raw with cigarette burns. She lay stunned, semi-conscious, roaming on the border of her pain.

Spared from an experiment, they had brought her to Mühsam's cell at the Commandant's suggestion that she would be goaded into attacking him (they were determined not to do their own killing), but the animal had sat down next to him, put her arms around his neck and smacked him a kiss on his cheek.

Surprised and delighted, Mühsam slipped into his cabaret manner. "Well, old girl," he said, "somebody's been giving you lessons in loving. What a couple we would make on the ballroom floor, Millie and me." What her name was, or if she had a name, we do not know. Mühsam called her Millie for its comic effect, teasing her animal nature, as human names applied to animals do, as if to explore the boundary between us and them.

He wrote his wife, Zensl, about the incident: "It was the kiss of death, for they have taken the animal and torture her for this. They want to drive me insane with her cries. No," he wrote, "they don't care whether I'm sane or not, they only want me to kill myself. What can I do? What should I do?" He crossed out the last line out of sympathy for Zensl, even though he was only writing the letter in his head.

They dragged him back to his cell with truncheons under his armpits. The other prisoners watched him with the intensity of a shared destiny. His footsteps--a shuffle in untied shoes, for his fingers had been broken and he could not knot his laces--was known--and why he was taken and where he went, for even prison life, and especially prison life, consumes itself in the social need for gossip; except for the Gypsy who kept himself apart with a wry disdain bred from the distrust of the "others," the ones who represented Europe, who "own it," as they say among themselves. The guards had left the Gypsy his clothes, his baggy pants and jacket, a striped shirt and stetson hat, and the medallion he wore around his neck.

A priest--a Cardinal--he was stripped of his robes--kept his eyes on the Bible he held in his hands--a ploy--for his eyes fluttered knowledgeably as Mühsam went by. Practiced in discretion he had less difficulty adjusting than Mühsam did, who succumbed to expressions of his old style buffoonery, a lifetime habit of escaping the self, or intensifying it by raising the pitch of rebuttal to folly; or Wyzanski, the young Polish communist, who still possessed vitality in spite of his beatings, and a self-protective self-righteousness which transformed his pain into argument. Anticlerical, he was suspicious of the Cardinal's presence in the prison. It represented a mockery to him, a tour-de-force. "The Pope will get him out," he said whenever occasion gave him the opportunity.

The Cardinal had at first been confined to a private room, on the recommendation of the Commandant, who respected his office and gave him a comfortable chamber, with a library, with a Louis Quatorze desk in it with the original inkstand on it, velvet drapes and a seventeenth century pianoforte, befitting one whose status had been created by fiat in the tenth century for members of the Roman aristocracy who otherwise would have had no place in the new Christian world. The Commandant also regarded it as a privilege of the ruling classes to create classes, the morphology and taxonomy of history.

Here the Cardinal had spent two years, deprived of little except his liberty (which did not surprise Wyzanski). He had a good bed to sleep on, satisfying food, wine with his meals, even visitors. (Like Mühsam, he had his allies.) Still, he wrote constantly to the Pope, not only regarding his imprisonment which he took to be fundamental to the issues, but regarding the issues. ("Surely, you are mistaken in thinking the fight against Bolshevism to be our primary struggle. You cannot engage in arguments about lesser and greater evils as other governments do.") In spite of his outspokenness against the German bishops who sympathized with Hitler, his imprisonment remained a token imprisonment--he conceded--but the whole world knew of it--and as such his imprisonment had the symbolic force of the tacit acceptance of the Vatican in the face of an opposition it would not--or could not--(in the end this difference was indistinguishable) contend with.

"I should like to know," he wrote the Papal secretary, "if you have some suggestion--practical or otherwise--in which civilized people can contend with the barbarities that are now abroad. I do not speak for myself. I am treated civilly (he wanted to write, "except for the interminable conversations I am forced to hold with the Commandant who finds my company 'enlightening'--his term, not mine.") but resisted any expressions that could give rise to interpretations of personal vexation.

"Believe us," the Papal officer responded, "when we say that we have your good permanently in our hearts and that your welfare is ever present to our souls."

If nothing further was said or done, it was felt that his imprisonment should be kept in perspective: he was not in morbid danger, he was not even in much discomfort.

The Cardinal did not see the matter in this way. A growing disillusionment with silence as a strategy--the sense that it formed his essential prison--made him write constantly. He filled boxes with "reflections" and wondered if they would ever be read or, if read, would make a difference. The continual scratching of his pen, hour after hour, struck him morbidly, and he would raise his head for breath, look around at the rococo ceiling above, angels in adoration, misplaced cupids, and write more furiously. He kept up such a torrent of letters--which finally found their way to the newspapers--that the Papal office sent a delegate to inquire after his condition.

"My condition!" he said, vexed, waving his hands over his rooms to the Papal delegate. "Do you mean my condition or the condition of my rooms? My rooms, as you see, are in excellent condition," and he waved his hand again at the velvet draperies and gold panels. "Perhaps you would like some wine and a canapé. I'll ring the guard to bring you some." His tone was not pleasant, but the delegate sat on a tapestried chair and said with restraint, "A cup of wine would be grand, thank you. As for the other matter, surely you see he is not at liberty to make a public statement."

The delegate's mood did not fit the Cardinal's: he exploded with anger. "He makes many public statements on other issues."

"Well, then, he cannot make them on all issues." The delegate dropped his chin and regarded his wine. "No one person can address himself to every issue. For some issues, silence, as the English say, is the better part of valor."

The Cardinal squinted his eyes, which gave him both an inquiring and a menacing expression. "Yes, and what then of the English?"

"You know the strength of the enemy. What are we to do? England will have to fight alone which, after all, is neither here nor there with respect to us."

The Cardinal threw his hands up. "Are there no Christians in England whose lives we should fear for?"

"We must certainly hope so."

The Cardinal could not restrain his exasperation any longer--two years of letter writing--but his exasperation was also neither here nor there, an irrelevancy, as they both knew, in the historical process to which the Church itself was now tied with less choice than either cared to calculate.

"Tell the Holy Father that for some of us his silences speak louder than his pronouncements."

"That may be," the delegate said, putting his cup of wine on the desk with an air of delicate conclusion, "but between the two, speech and silence, nothing is more discreet than silence," and he left. "I regret," he soon wrote the Cardinal, "that the Holy Father has no practical suggestions to make at this time, concerning those issues which you so feelingly raise and which we ourselves acknowledge with our full hearts. Be assured that the conflicts of Europe are foremost in our thoughts and that we do always plead for pity, mercy, compassion, and that the nations will be enlightened in their duties toward one another. We pray for brotherly love and faith abundant among all the nations, but of those practical suggestions of which you spoke, we are not at liberty to regard them, but be assured of our love and our faith and our continual prayers for your welfare."

The Commandant knocked on the door, and entered before the Cardinal responded. "I am sorry it is a disappointment to you," he said, referring to the letter. It did not surprise the Cardinal that the Commandant knew its contents. "A matter of time," he murmured in response, preferring loyalty under the circumstances.

"Of course, what else?" the Commandant said, eyeing the letter left open on the desk. "But I trust it brought you some comfort, at least. If it says less than you hoped for, perhaps it was never meant to fulfill expectations." He sighed in a fully civil way as one performing an act of condolence. "You know I used to sing in a church choir," he said, as if to extenuate his expressions of understanding, and he sat down at the pianoforte and began to play some Bach, Jesu, Joy of Man's Desiring, so well that even the Cardinal, after a while and against his better judgment ("After all," the Commandant once said to him, "you aggrandized so much of the land of Europe in your appetite for spirit, you made the rise of the secular nations a necessity in Europe's struggle against religious tyranny.")--was impressed. Noticing the effect he made, the Commandant continued, "I haven't forgotten my training," and he bent his ear to the pianoforte, appraising the notes as if they were jewels. He admired the Cardinal, and it pleased him to play for him, but when he made his mind up to it, he could resist flattery, though he was haunted by a desire for it. His chief source of gratification was in the company he kept, even in the company of his prisoners. He was addicted--he described himself this way--to good conversation, "enlightening conversation," of which he was deprived for the most part, under these circumstances, except for Mühsam, who was loquacious--but unfortunately an anarchist and a socialist and a Jew; while the Cardinal at least was none of these, least of all what the Commandant disliked more than another--an upstart. What the Cardinal's personal background was--he was the son of a bank clerk--was beside the point: he belonged to the class of Cardinals and existed within the rhythm and pattern of Europe while the cult of individualism--anarchism--socialism--bohemianism--"modern" Jewry, in a word Mühsam, were hurling stones against it. If only for reasons of snobbery, the Commandant's sympathies were with lineage and form.

But his respect for the Cardinal's office was alloyed with triumph: the "true" mark of respect. He closed the cover to the pianoforte precipitously, looked at his wristwatch to remind himself of an appointment, and said, "Really! Art is a whore. You know as well as I do anyone can play Bach if he has had enough training."

"What an enemy of our own making," the Cardinal thought after he left. ("Yes," he wrote, "you inquire after my condition, and how can I convey to you that what you call my condition is not anything you can see with your eyes.") He sat at his desk and looked out through the French doors into the garden and the grounds surrounding the fortress, where he often watched the Commandant do his morning exercises amid a flutter of peacocks and wild turkeys.

The land was level for several acres, covered with moss and grass and pathways trailing vines, orchids, phlox, until it fell down a slope where the villagers let their sheep run and the unsuspecting townspeople lived in a concentric circle of houses surrounding their modest church. The fortress grounds were open to them on holidays and they came in family groups, not suspecting the prisons that lay beneath the solid buildings. If they saw the Cardinal standing in the French doors, why would they suspect that he was held prisoner here? The Commandant depended upon his never saying so.

It was this idea, long recognized and now ripened with apprehension, that made the Cardinal change his course of action the next morning.

The Commandant came out as usual to take his four mile jog around the grounds. His servant emerged too, carrying a towel and cologne. Watching him do his exercises, the Cardinal experienced a sequence of insights, begun the night before, which made him pace his room, made him unfit to go on staying there. The Commandant passed his view every four minutes, his body inclined so right as he rounded the trail, the turkeys and peacocks scattering to the side of him. It was the ripeness of this manner, sustained only by its form, needing only to appear upon the scene in one uniform or another, in this setting or a similar one, that was oppressive--the affinities between them--their parallel lines traversing the greenswards of Europe--the beauty of the places--the gardens of camellias--the pools of delight--the mists of morning caught in the weeping willows--was painful to behold--the beloved beauty of the place--the walks--the fountains streaming silver in the sunlight--so valued even by the townspeople who enjoyed it on special occasions. Who had built this place? What cruel, seducing, lascivious architect had dreamed this prison? "Why should I blame him anymore than myself?" the Cardinal thought, pacing the floor. "What, after all, is the difference if, in the end, one belongs to a collection of things, becomes a jewel in this setting or another?"

Still, he shrank from doing anything which might seem histrionic, out of character--he hated flamboyance but, how else, under the circumstances, act? There was so little room for maneuvers. He could think of little else to do. Finally, though it was not his nature to do it, he removed his robes and folded them on the desk, feeling cheapened by the act it took to become holy. He called the guard in and saw at once the effect his nakedness had. Speechless, the guard turned on his heels and ran to tell the Commandant, even interrupting his exercises.

The Cardinal watched them though his window. The Commandant's eyes fluttered in his direction, a heavy lidded but piercing glance. He couldn't see through the glass--the sun was reflecting in it--but the Cardinal could see him hesitate--think with the very muscles of his face--query himself whether this was one of those times to interrupt his exercises. Apparently, yes. The Commandant put his jacket back on--but not with his customary air of having brought the morning to an agreeable finish. The Cardinal experienced a half regretful pang of victory. It fortified him just enough to withstand the look of repulsion the Commandant gave him when he arrived in his room and looked at him in his underclothes, turned on his heels and said to the guards, "Take him where he wants to go."

Having inched his mind this far forward as to experience a new found level of unholiness in his doubts, of longing to go back on his own actions, against which he had to summon his resolve not to betray himself, the Cardinal shouted after him, "I'm entitled to the same prison as everyone else."

The Commandant came on occasion to visit him in his new prison, quite obviously to gauge the effects of the new surrounding on the Cardinal. "It doesn't matter," he said to the Cardinal, "even if you become a martyr or a saint, it will not change one thing. Everything is too far gone. You know that yourself."

The Cardinal proved to be as tenacious as the Commandant, and theirs became a battle of wills fought on an invisible principle. "You are probably right," the Cardinal said, "but even facts change sometimes." Months of this kind of imprisonment had made his face sallow and fleshless, like a death mask revealing the salient features. Within the confines of his new cell, he performed Mass every day and the Gypsy and Wyzanski joined him, making symbolic signals across their cells from which ritual movements had been stripped to the elemental communion, after which the Gypsy slid back into his hostility and suspicion of things European, and Wyzanski took up his anticlerical stand. "The Pope will get him out," he said, contemptuous of the Cardinal's prison life, this not-believable trespass into the political domain.

Besides them, there were some others, all political prisoners of various shades: a Millenarist by the name of Vilhelm, who was equally as tenacious as the communist and the Cardinal. He belonged to a sect without church, without organization, "without hierarchy," he said, lifting his sparsely bearded chin in the direction of the Cardinal, "only with Jesus"; and with a set of tenets which apparently had sustained them for centuries, confirmed in the Second Coming, enduring a spiritual hunger for it which made everything else in life dull for them. They lived like the Gypsies, disdainful of the schools, the governments, the museums, the institutions, that had been erected on "God's land," which ought not to have anything on it but animal, plant and vegetable life and the minimum constructions for shelter. As if shot out of history, certainly out of its contemporary terms--progress, technology, realpolitick, diplomacy, negotiations---every morning he wrote on the back wall of his cell, "Jesus Saves," and placed his Bible in his lap. Every morning the guards beat him for it and erased it. Sometimes, a guard hesitated before the writing with a superstitious dread. Vilhelm, quick to note this and dreading nothing himself, pounced on the man with an onslaught of evangelism surprising in its imprisoned energy, inspiring panic in the guard that something had been found out about him, something that ought not to have been found out, like plague or disease, and he increased Vilhelm's punishment.

Wyzanski, intrigued by Vilhelm, argued on his behalf that he "represented the original intentions of communism." ("He is always looking for religious justification," Mühsam wrote Zensl) and answered Wyzanski with the touch of hilarity he always felt in the presence of nonsense: "Wyzanski, you should know better. Communism is about workers and workers are about buildings and construction, history in a word, the state, etc. Remember Hegel said there is no history without the state. Vilhelm is against all that. What he wants is subsistence. Marx never wanted subsistence for the worker. In Vilhelm's state, everybody shares nothing except the spiritual kingdom. In Marx's state, everybody shares everything, and he couldn't care less about the spiritual kingdom. Do you think Jesus could come after Marx?" ("A good piece of nonsense from an intelligent person brings you back to life," he wrote Zensl. "Outside of a cabaret in Berlin, I have the best companions here. The Cardinal is a first rate fellow and not an antisemite. The communist says he's not an antisemite, but he is. He thinks because he is anticlerical he is not antisemitic, and that his religion will save him from going to hell. He thinks he has the best of both worlds. Ha! Ha! Ha! If only I had a cigarette for the proper effect of that laugh--a little smoke rising from the lips gives a man a very clever look.")

"Then what is he imprisoned for?" Wyzanski laughed with his characteristic note of contemptuous challenge.

Vilhelm did not undertake to answer for himself. He revealed nothing except the scheme of his faith, not because he was secretive, but because he had nothing else to reveal. There was no progression to his ideas and he had nothing to embroider. Many found him monotonous and taciturn, as certainly the Commandant did. Some regarded him as a "throwback"--to what they could not say. But most confronted him with disbelief and left him alone, though he meant what he said, what they had heard said most of their lives in other contexts. Vilhelm's problem was that he never meant anything else.

Mühsam whetted Wyzanski's appetite for combat--it was the Jewish socialist in Mühsam that did it. "I'm not a communist," Mühsam said, determined to keep the differences between himself and Wyzanski clear. "What's the difference?" Wyzanski laughed at him across the corridor space of their cells.

"You'll find out," Mühsam hoarsely whispered back.

"What did they arrest you for?" Wyzanski laughed challengingly. "Hey, tell me that, for being a socialist or for being a communist?"

They had so much in common--even Mühsam confessed it--but rubbed each other the wrong way. "Pity," Mühsam said, "you don't know the difference. What's that got to do with anything? They can imprison me, but I still make the distinctions between good and evil. Anyway, I'm here on about twelve different charges. Think of that! Pacifism, antimilitarism, socialism, anarchism, bohemianism, feminism, Jewishism, and even for writing poetry about Jesus." He counted the charges off on his fingers with theatrical aplomb.

"I don't blame them for arresting you for that," Wyzanski said. "What does Jesus have to do with you, hey?"

Mühsam lay down on his cot and regarded Wyzanski with overt irony. "Why not?" he said, " a fellow Jew caught on the loom of history. What's Jesus to you?"

Wyzanski's answer shot out of him as if he had been waiting for someone to ask him that. "A fellow communist like me."

Mühsam whistled and laughed. ("Really, Zensl, a man could do worse than go to his execution with these, ha, ha, ha.") He did not write his laughter out--how could he?--and he erased the line altogether, on second thought (Zensl would not be prepared for it), but he wrote her about his cellmates, "his boon companions in destiny;" for her sake he composed a scenario on "his prison cabaret," for her entertainment--and wrote it out in his old style, seizing the energy of it, the electric communion between entertainer and audience that had been a magnetic field between them, so powerful an attraction they had for each other, entertainer and audience, no other audience like them, poets, intelligentsia, members of the Dada movement, bohemians in the Grün Deutschland movement, "Die Konnenden," political cranks all, "the Coming Ones," as they called themselves, bound for the future together. Even the ones who came to heckle him proved the power of his style---legs astride a chair--standing in a pool of light--cigarette in mouth--body cheapened with poverty and poor living, too many prisons, not enough food--words biting holes in the air as decisive as gems--valuable.

"Berlin! Ha! Berlin has everything but human nature.

Now, Paris, there's a city. Paris lives, Berlin functions."

"Bismarxism!" he said. "Exactly, I said, "the worst of both worlds. They arrested me for this."

"Come," Wyzanski said, 'they arrested you for being Jewish."

"Oh, of course, that, as if that's all I was."

"Mühsam. You know my name. Mühsam. Means arduous in German."

He was always pleased by this fact. "Makes too much of it," Else Lasker-Schüler said. "He will wind up in front of a firing squad or hanging from a tree," and nicknamed him "wilde Jude,"--because of his red beard and his poetry, but mainly because of his politics. "Look out for yourself, Mühsam," she warned him, sitting in their cabaret, done up in her gaudy, freaky poverty, a feather in her hair "to symbolize hope." Good friend, she had come to his rescue before with protest letters and petitions, when he had been imprisoned with Toller and Landauer and Leviné. "Good friend and fellow poet," she warned him, "now you are free, Mühsam, stay away from politics. What has a poet to do with politics? Stay away, Mühsam. Stop writing satires and write your visions. A poet can sooner create a world than create a state."

"They're the same," he said, and wrote his essay, Die Befreiung der Gesellschaft Stat. "I never knew how to separate them--the earthly Jerusalem and the heavenly Jerusalem--the world--humanity--God--where politics left off and religion began. That's how I see Jesus."

"Whatever else Jesus and Marx have in common," the Cardinal said to Wyzanski, "one believed in God the Father and the other did not, make what you will of the difference."

Mühsam sank his head back on his pillow. "What is the difference now? Calvary is all around us--there is so much political retrogression--I think worse than at any other time. The whole world is now Golgotha. Yes,

Mühsam means arduous in German. What's history without passion? I took my name for a symbol."

"German?" they asked me.

"Yes, sir, a thousand years."

"Born?"

My father should live so long.

"His occupation?"

"Pharmacist."

"Put down Jew."

"Right."

"Religion?"

"That doesn't concern you."

"Write Jewish," they said.

"Right, be a Jew at home and a German abroad."

My father should live so long.

He wrote it out satirically, the whole of it, the history of his generation--Der Konnenden--stuffed into cabarets and cells--the anarchists, the socialists, the barefooted soldiers (the others, the practitioners of realpolitick, knew what it was all about--how to fight the enemy--how to prepare for war--how to prepare for peace--how to negotiate terms--they knew) or, if you prefer, he wrote it out in the new style of prophecy--eerily, in which he foretold how his civilization would be carried to its death in a modern invention of its own making:

Onward, onward without rest
to the north, east, south, west!
Seek, soul seek!....
See your life flash by in pain
From the window of a midnight train.
Shriek, soul, shriek!

and foretold the style of his death:

An aging corpse
Hangs from a telegraph pole.
His dangling legs reached out--to--
Oh! can it catch them, for pity's sake--
The outspread branches of an oak tree

("Thank god for the innocent things of nature," he wrote Zensl. "Will they ever vindicate us--or trust us again?") The vision scared him into wilder satire. "Yes, arduous, that is my name, also called wilde Jude by my closer friends. Don Quijote, and romantic anarchist, antimilitarist, pacifist (arrested as a conscientious objector the first time), feminist and yes, vegetarian, "a political crank" some said--you know who--those who know the world better than he did, the realpolitikniks. ("Now, I ask you, Zensl, what is the difference and how could it be otherwise?") "We bohemians," he wrote for the newspapers fond of articles about that type of life, "play with the accidents of time the better to approach eternity."

What did they understand--his audience? His performances were combats in which he struggled with forces--Europe--history--antisemitism. (Kafka wrote, "They forgive the Jewish communist and the Jewish socialist nothing.")

"What is your religion?" the Commandant asked.

"Humanity."

"Put down Jew, non-professing."

"Right you are."

He struggled with the New Germany--the poor--with mankind. For laughter.

"...Ein Jude zog aus Nazareth
Die Armen glücklich zu machen

Applause! Applause! Applause for this man with the wild beard who lives on cigarette smoke. Yes! Thank you very much. Pass the hat around. Enough for a meal tonight. Jerusalem who stoneth her prophets! And Berlin and Paris! Now, what do you think, mein heer Berliner? Who has driven out more prophets, Jerusalem or you? But for you it will not matter--you will never miss them.

("Now, Zensela, I tell you, my companion, the communist from Poland, wears a crucifix around his neck and when I said to him once, 'I'm surprised you wear that,' it touched him wrong, as if he thought I was deriding his communist faith. 'What can a Jew understand,' he answered back at once--hoopla! flavoring his idealism with a little contempt--the parsley in the soup.

Of course,' I whispered through the bars, 'quite right. Of course! The gulf is very deep, very deep, but not so deep here,' and I pushed some of my poetry through the bars at him. You know the ones. About the Eucharist. 'Here the gulf narrows,' I said to him. 'After all, all prisoners have something in common. I too think of Jesus as my kindred spirit.' And what do you think he did when I said this. He roared at me like a Polish communist imitating a bulldog, 'Judenschwein!'

'Look out,' I said, 'I'm glad you wear the crucifix, but be careful they don't choke you with it. From me you have nothing to fear. It concentrates my absorption into history. But be careful about the others. Do you know what is the most difficult thing in history?--who knows--maybe it's the original historical problem--to know who your enemy is--for the enemy will not identify himself--he does not come out and say, hey, I am the enemy, and takes his bow on the stage.'

'Shut up, Mühsam,' someone shouted at me. Foolishly, I thought it was one of the other prisoners and ran off at the mouth. Zensele, my love, no one put up with me as you did. But it was a guard and he came and took my pencil and paper away. Yes, he took my pencil and paper away, but I write this with my mind to you. Zensl, be well. Know that whatever you hear of me, it will not be true. For your sake, for the sake of our love, for the sake of the Jew in me, know that I will never take my own life. Do not believe it, if you hear it.")

The prisoners' eyes followed him as the guards took him from his cell. Their bodies jerked with the manic restlessness that pervades prisoners with no place to go. They whispered to him in voices of deadly irony meant for sympathy: "This is what comes of holding out, Mühsam."

"Don't worry for me," he laughed, "I'm used to prisons." He made a face at them, exaggerating the effects of his missing parts, ears, teeth, rotten gums, broken nose. "I'm no novice. Niederschonenfeld, 1924. Sonnenburg, Brandenburg, Oranienburg. Don't worry for me." His eyes were white in a face of crazy colors, swollen blue lips, swollen purple nose, red scars where his ears had been torn off, red hair and beard dirty with lice, rotted gray gums, fingers blackened, twisted and broken.

("Don't worry for me," he wrote his wife, "you know I've been in prison before. I'm no novice. I shall always get word to you. Thank God for bribery. What would we poor prisoners do without this corruption. Or history do without prisoners who escape to tell the world. Thank God for errors and mistakes. That is what we wretches will have to cling to in the future. Blessed be the loopholes. Erich Mühsam, leader of the loophole. 'Look at him,' the Commandant said, when they first arrested me. 'Look at him. This is your famous leader of the Munich Ratrepublick, this scarecrow, this judenshwein, this target in a shooting gallery, this rooster with the red beard.'

'Yes,' I said to them when they put me against the wall to shoot me, I tore off my eyeguards and said, 'Shoot, I want to see the bastards who shoot me, Mühsam, whose name means arduous in German.'

This is what they do, Zensl. They tell me they will execute me on such and such a day, and they march me out and then they march me in. They think they will frighten me to death with make-believe. They think I will die of pretenses.")

He paused at Vilhelm's cell, his eyes blistered red. "My poor animal," he said to him, "do you know what they are doing to her."

Vilhelm did not answer. Only iron survives. Only the spirit. Only the spirit that is iron.

"Be strong," Wyzanski whispered. "Give them nothing. Nothing!"

The guards tightened their truncheons under Mühsam's armpits and pulled him away. The Commandant waited in the library for him, a sign of the respect he bore the poet--he had taken the trouble to look at his poetry--which he disliked. Still he knew that Mühsam was a journalist, a writer, one of the haute Juden intelligentsia, and a Berliner, a man who was held in esteem by many, though mostly of his own kind, bohemian rabble, people who think it clever to walk barefoot, to imitate poverty. Such people irritated his fastidious habits--a trait that was as much a part of his thinking as his dressing and which passed into his historical perspective. How could they convince a man with two dozen different dress uniforms and three personal tailors. Nudity destroys history.

Two of his tailors were Jewish, of course, for Jewish tailors were the best of the kind--there was a special competence about them. He felt this in how their tape measures drooped around their necks, handled briskly, the ends worn with years of use, the pins held precariously between their lips defying their patterns of speech, a regular barrage of humming and comments in spite of the pins which moved up and down in their moving mouths, kept there as skillfully as a laborer keeps his feet on a catwalk, and the chalk markers behind their ears as professional looking as an accountant's pencil. His other tailor--a Lutheran--stuck him once and exclaimed with pain on his behalf. Not Rosenbloom or Rosenberg. They moved accurately. A special knowingness in their manner. A special knowingness of things, an historic competence about goods. Which did make you wonder, as the Führer once said--one of his milder speculations as far as the Commandant was concerned, for he disliked his speeches--found them hysterical declarations proclaiming the Third Reich as "inheriting" the future. This was a false note in the logic of things; it irritated him. "Really," he said to a fellow officer, raising an eyebrow with critical distaste, "he has no sense of history."

"Don't you believe him?" the fellow officer asked surprised, very surprised, even querulous, for to disbelieve that was to disbelieve the whole enterprise.

"It's a good slogan," the Commandant said. They came down the steps of a Ministry. He looked up at the sun, as he always did when he emerged from a building, testing the lint on his glasses, "but, after all, a contradiction. One never inherits the future. One can only inherit the past. You can prepare for the future, yes--by inheriting the past. Ah, ha!" He was pleased with himself.

They stopped midway down the steps, appropriately against a noble sweep of concrete stairway. "Come," his companion said, relaxing, "do you think the Führer should have said, 'let us inherit the past?'"

The Commandant was taken aback by a confusion of thought. He wrinkled his brow. They burst out laughing together and continued down the steps. "Lucky they don't ask me to make speeches," he said cavalierly.

"Deprive them of needle and thread," he thought, eyeing himself in the three way mirror, "and they'll come undone." (He meant the Jews, for his respect and contempt for them were mixed in equal proportions.) He took first one posture, then another to see how the suit wrinkled and behaved as he moved this way and that. He had learned that the worst way to test the fit of a suit was to stand like a mannikin in front of a mirror. Therefore, he bent, he stretched, he strode, he moved about and the three tailors moved with him, pins in mouth, tape measure around their necks. He eyed himself, they eyed him, studying his form in all its postures, actually a format rather than a form. There never was such an extraordinary case of learned lineage. It was as if the maxims of a mother--walk with your head erect--keep your chest high--do not let your shoulders droop--worked as well for impressing heads of states as for a finishing school. People succumb to the proper mode oftener than to the Sermon on the Mount.

It surprised the Commandant to discover how universally this was so. The son of an insurance agent, he had no reason to know it and discovered it accidentally. He simply noticed it was so while sitting in a train one afternoon, waiting for it to start. He was gazing absentmindedly through the window of his private carriage, his head on his gloved hand, his military hat cocked over his eye, looking fortuitously moody, like a Renaissance prince by Michaelangelo. An accident, but the look stuck. Every woman who went by gazed back at him. Several even gazed back as if their heads turned against their will, as if their eyes were being moved by a magnetic field between themselves and him. He must be impressive! He could not escape the conclusion. So many people looked at him. A press photographer went by on the prowl, walked up and down the platform, waiting for a war or a suicide, and finally came to his carriage. The Commandant's career began here.

"May I?" the reporter asked, and took his picture. "I represent the---. Tell me, Commandant, in a few words--I know the train is about to start--what do you think of the situation in Poland? Do you think there will be a war? Can you comment on the economy? What's the meaning of the military maneuvers on the border? Is there anything important happening in France? Do you wish to make a statement about your recent promotion? Is it true that you had an organ placed in Oranienburg and will have Bach concerts there?"

The Commandant ruminated, among the many questions which one to address himself to. "Yes," he said, "I am a lover of Bach. His music is good for my nerves--so many irritating things these days."

"Does that mean that you are dismissing Wagner?" the reporter asked, quick to sense a possible dissension.

"Dismissing Wagner?" the Commandant said with soft irony and an equally soft twinkle in his eye, to dispel the ludicrous interpretation that his personal tastes--anyone's personal tastes--could have anything to do with history--a sign of humility, or geniality. "How can one dismiss Wagner?"

The effect was the opposite of humility: it was grandiose. Several mysteries knocked about in the reporter's head in the form of further questions, but the train began to move. "Thank you very much, mein herr Commandant," he said. "May I take another picture?"

The Commandant fidgeted. Photographs were always such a gamble, particularly newspaper pictures, as if the subject were taken "on the run," mouth open, caught in a stammer. But his picture (he had reason to be forever grateful to the reporter) caught him like a portrait, elbow on the windowsill, head leaning on his gloved hand, thoughtful and authoritative, the angle of his hat, l'angle juste, as if he had posed for an oil to be hung alongside the oils he now had in his private gallery, robed men who never looked hasty but always historical, composed within and without.

This was the Commandant's greatest asset: composure, recognized as such by those around him, so employable to history, so useful to convey legitimacy. In the archives he can still be seen to this effect, a little to the left

of the Führer, a foot or two behind him with an air of readiness (like a servant to the gods?) and that air of lineage so employable to the historical moment lending to the group in the picture the claim it made, the indispensable claim, that he had come to inherit the past.

These are the only assets that matter, that can take you anywhere, at any time, in any age--as a knight or a courtier, a duke or a cardinal, one who stands in the background as a consort to rulers. Composure and calm. But they will get you nowhere as a merchant, a trader, a bricklayer or bookseller, a mechanic, an artist or a writer.

However, though satisfied with himself as he had reason to be, it was so easy to dissatisfy him. He was so perfect and so worried. A flaw--a crease--a wrinkle--and his lips tightened critically.

"What is this?" he asked, bending down to examine his cuff. "What do you sew here?" he asked Rosenbloom.

A crease of warning crossed the tailor's forehead. "Your uniform," he said carefully, " mein herr Commandant."

"And if I call you a liar!" he said, as he looked into the mirror at his offending reflection. "These Jews!" he thought. "Yes, a liar!" he said out loud, "for you know very well you are sewing something else."

Rosenbloom paused with the needle in one hand and fingered the thread in his other, like Ariadne. "To be sure, mein Commandant," he said, pulling the offending cuff into place, "I sew history. Here, I have straightened it out."

"That's better, yes. It looked foolish before, the way you had it, like a dog's ear flapping loosely," he said peevishly (a quality only his tailors knew about him), still critically eyeing himself, his trouser, as if the cuff might

change back again to a demeaning flip flop. "Yes, it seems to have straightened itself out. Well, you are a genius, after all. What shall I do without you?"

Rosenbloom bowed, acknowledging the compliment. "You are too kind. The world is full of tailors. The Chinese have some remarkable ones."

"But not like you Jews."

The Lutheran pinched his eye with envy. "If you like the compliment, you may take it," Rosenbloom whispered to him, bowing out of the room. But there was nothing he could say to console the Lutheran for the slight. Struggle as the Lutheran might and have faith as he said he did, the slight was enough. The Jews always seemed to be ahead.

The Commandant waved them all away and went out to meet Mühsam in his library, a room surprisingly filled with Jewish books--stocked like a pond with carp: Bibles and Talmuds, Commentaries and Responsa, Tractates, Treatises, Medieval philosophers and poets, Mishnas, Gemaras and Kabbalahs. A staff of twenty worked daily reading them, and reported to him whatever of interest took their minds, and from their reports he made reports to the Führer. His library had other material in it too, of course, journals and periodicals of the last fifty or seventy-five years and a valuable collection of pornography. His own preferred reading was newspapers--which he read voraciously (and for relaxation, fashion magazines, a habit he had inherited from his mother).

He chose this room for his interview with Mühsam, for its effect: he wanted him to know he respected his literary talents, even his Jewishness (though not, of course, his anarchism, socialism, bohemianism, individualism, antimilitarism, liberalism, feminism, modernism), and chose a copy of Judah Halevi to hold in his hand, a symbol of his respect and his regrets.

("Zensl, my love! remember only this. They could not make me take my life. If you hear that I am dead, they killed me. Their sole aim is to make me do their dirty work. This is a distinction they keep in mind, and so do I.")

"A co-religionist of yours," the Commandant said, laying the book conspicuously on his desk.

"A fellow poet."

The Commandant paused with his hand still over the book, caught in mid-flight, not sure if Mühsam intended an impertinence. "Is he not a co-religionist?"

"I only mean to say we have many things in common."

Ah! an evasion: "Yes, but you are forever denying the main point. The Führer has nothing against the Judaic religion."

(Ha, ha, ha!") "Neither do I. My grandfather----"

"Yes, your grandfather! Exactly." To Mühsam's surprise there was pique in the Commandant's voice. "That is why the Jewish people have decayed."

"Well, as for that. Surely not without company." ("Wily Jew," the Commandant thought, the thought dancing in his eyes, lightening with irritability.) "All history is decline," Mühsam said, "a regular mythology of decline." (He could not resist the look in the Commandant's eye: it compelled him to put his head on the block.) "I tell you what--I would have preferred, I mean me, personally, as a Jew" (he paused slightly, smiled slightly), "if you will permit me to say so, I would have preferred myself to have been a soldier in Caesar's army than a soldier at any other time."

The Commandant felt he was being baited--and by a man who had his head on the block. It did not soothe his nerves. "Perhaps you think Germans are not as good as Romans?" The patriotic note was sounded to suit a purpose, for the Commandant only wanted Mühsam to curtsey.

("I would like once," he wrote to Zensl, "to construct a sentence utterly at my command, from which nothing can be extracted but what I allow. To control a single sentence, to send it out into the world and nail it against its forehead.") "In many things better," he said.

"Wily Jew," the Commandant thought again, but not entirely with denigration, more with impatience and his constant irritability, for the thought was a component of the respect he felt for him, the reason, after all, why he chose his company for conversation (along with the Cardinal's) and not someone like Vilhelm. The Gypsy was never considered.

Loquaciousness was Mühsam's rotten luck, an obsession with telling the world what was wrong with it. The Commandant walked about the room--the Jewish section of it--twenty shelves or more of books, from floor to ceiling, esoteric titles that had ceased to mean anything to most--The Sayings of the Fathers, The Attributes of God, The Twelve Expressions of Mercy, and so on. "Really," he said, incredulous at the carelessness of things in his own library, and ran his finger along a rim of dust. He held it up to Mühsam and said again, "Really!" and dismissed him.

They took him back briefly to his cell and told him to get ready. They did not tell him what for, or how he should prepare himself. He knew what for. Everyone on the floor knew, and their spirits stiffened with resistance. The Gypsy inhaled a piercing breath which whistled in his ribs. He looked about with an air of searching, a random movement signifying a state of mind without an object, then he moved away towards the wall of his cell as if he had found what he was looking for--the sense, at least if only that, of moving away: an ineffectual act, for the animal's screams penetrated the walls and the prisoners were seized with a restlessness that drove them beserk, an amorphousness of physical energy as if the biological foundation of life were cut loose from social meaning and usefulness, and became a motion venemously random and nervous. They banged on their bar cells with their tin cups and shouted to drown out the animal's screams.

Wyzanski's anticlericalism bit him like a shark. He turned on the Cardinal. "You! A man of God! Why don't you do something? Why doesn't the Pope do something? Why don't you speak out?"

("I will shout with you," the Cardinal thought). He merely said, "Ssshhh," more or less to comfort.

"What can the Pope do?" Mühsam said. "It would embarrass him to speak out. That is why he keeps quiet."

As if he had skins to shed, Wyzanski came to the defense of the clergy. "You are anti- Christian," he said.

"Mühsam is right," the Cardinal said.

"Yes, it would embarrass Europe," Mühsam said, laboring with the difficulty of putting on his shoes with broken fingers. "Do you think the Commandant will listen to him--or to the Führer? The Pope's silence will be his strength in the future. Many books will be written about why he kept silent. Better books than the embarrassment of impotence." He struggled with the second shoe. "I do not speak of the present pope. My argument is not ad hominem. I speak of the class of popes, the genre of popes. Although formerly they used to speak out, now they keep quiet."

"Ha! I always knew it," Wyzanski said, "at bottom, you are against us."

"He is right," the Cardinal said again. "Perhaps we no longer have the language."

"Yes," Mühsam said, and pushed his feet the rest of the way into their shoes, "you have no new thing to say to me." He looked down at his feet, the exhaustive job of getting them into shoes with broken fingers. "I am tired of your hatred. What does it signify, here, after all?" He shuffled out of his cell and the guards brought him to the room where the chimpanzee was kept. They strapped him into a chair, around the waist and bound his hands and feet. "Even if you shut your eyes," they said to him, "you will hear her scream."

("Zensela--I have not slept since--maybe I do sleep because I seem to dream--but then I seem not to sleep, only to hear her cries--I have not slept a whole night.") Those were among his last words to her. ("There is too much darkness when I lay down. I cannot sleep. Zensela, my girl, try to be brave--it is a fact that tonight I find the darkness to be too much. I do not wish to crawl out of the cave--there is too much political retrogression everywhere--and no end in sight.")

"It will not do you any good to shut your mind away," the guard said. "You know that she is suffering. You can hear her."

("Yes, I wish to suffer with her. Can you believe this?") His chin dropped on his chest. Tears fell from his eyes, which he would have preferred to be invisible from the notice of the guards, but they jerked his head up. Dimly, he heard his fellow prisoners banging on their cell bars, Wyzanski, Vilhelm, the Cardinal. They did their best to drown out the noise, but he heard her screams anyway.

She was skinned alive. Her suffering nerves and the cortical knot of her spine were exposed and she entered the history of the human race slowly, this creature of trees and vines and forest life, whose ancestors had been born in a time when there was no more mercy than at another time, but there was more justice; when logos meant law and law meant the boundary between permissible acts and acts which cut man off from the sight of God, for from Noah to Jesus man was sinful but redeemable, but from Jesus to now he has become abhorrent and unredeemable.

She who stopped short of being human in the evolutionary scale, who never walked the halls of a museum, never listened to a lecture in science about her nature, never wrote exegesis on the Bible, never worried what divinity meant, or if the Gospels and the white man had improved upon the lesser breeds, whom the Encyclopedia describes as "educable" and "capable of insight," whose instincts had been created to trust, fell out of the hand of God into the hand of man and became a mass of mutilated flesh in a corner, a tuft of fur left on her back erect with terror--the last sign of her life. The eyes she fixed upon the world were put out with a burning rod, and then she belonged forever to the night of human things.

They took Mühsam back to his cell. His feet shuffled in their untied shoes. ("Zensela, let me say it once, let me betray my instinct for life this once--let me falter once--I will pick myself up again and go on.") He stopped at

Vilhelm's cell and peered through the bars at him. Vilhelm's head drooped into his shoulders. He did not look up. Mühsam's eyes drifted to the back wall of the cell. "Saves what?" he asked. Vilhelm's head sunk lower. "The world," he whispered. But then, daunted, conceded by adding in a low voice, "They shall reap the whirlwind."

Mühsam could not hold back his tears. They fell wantonly, liberated from a stone that had burst open. "The Jesus I know would have settled for less," he whispered back. His tears broke his resistance. Faster than his guards thought he could still move on his legs--irony and grief gave him such wings--he dropped to his knees and wept. "The hangman's bread is passed to us in this cellar, bless this blood that from the body flows from my poor animal in terror. Can you pray for her soul? Can you pray for her soul?" He banged his forehead on the floor. "Can you pray for her soul?"

We, in the outside world, when we heard of this event--the torture of an animal to drive a prisoner to suicide--wondered why there was no argument that Mühsam--the others--the Cardinal--could have made to prevent it. Had they all passed then, truly, into a place where neither religion nor poetry availed? It is hard to imagine it--that so unyielding a state of things beyond the reach of the civilization we had carefully built and trusted was all that was left.

Mühsam struggled all night to sleep. He wrapped his arms over his head to shut out the light. Not his fingers only, but all his bones felt broken. Wyzanski watched him struggle and wanted to call to him, but the Cardinal signaled to him not to. "What can we do for him that sleep cannot?"

("My heart is broken," he wrote Zensl, "at last. It is over, at least for that.") He searched in his cot for a place to put his broken body, and turned his face to the wall. Its clammy stone was familiar to him, the touch of his wormy blanket. ("Zensela, place a stone somewhere for her and, if you can, put her name on it. I must try to sleep--an hour or two before the next interrogation.")

"Name?"

"Mühsam--means arduous in German."

"Religion?"

"Non-professing."

"Put down Jew."

"Right you are."

"Religion? Why don't you tell us what your religion is?"

"Yes, I will tell you now. I have kept it a secret all these years. Only now that the animal is dead, I will tell you. Rahamanim bene rahamanim."

"Why don't you speak your native language, Mühsam?"

"That is my native language."

"What is your nationality, Mühsam? You speak like a foreigner."

"Yes, I am a foreigner. I and my religion and my nationality and my language. We are foreigners in your world."

But there were no more interrogations. Mühsam was found hanged from a beam on the outside wall of the fortress, near an oak tree that grew there. ("Remember, Zensl, if you hear that I have committed suicide, do not believe it. The force of life in me is greater than the force of death. I can withstand anything but them. If you hear that I am dead, know that they killed me.") He heard in his last moments, when all other explanations were silent and none were about to tell him of the future of the world, he heard the voice of God, as Job had heard it: Behold, behemoth, which I made with thee, and Leviathan, whose eyes are like the eyelids of the morning. What is man that he should destroy my creatures and contend with me. He has his day, but I have eternity, and I will give you creation forever as a consolation for this moment.

Mühsam's body was given to Zensl for burial in Berlin-Dahlem on July 16, 1934, and many of his friends--those who were not in hiding--attended the funeral. There are official records about all this (including a memo from the Commandant about Mühsam's "suicide")--but not about the chimpanzee. Wyzanski escaped and told about her. The Gypsy was castrated and then killed, or killed first and then castrated. Vilhelm's tongue was torn out by its roots by the Commandant in a fit of rage; and the Cardinal was later released--as Wyzanski knew he would be--but he became an ambiguous figure, acclaimed and then forgotten and, no longer remembered, deprived of the authority of his singular behavior, not sure if he was in the foreground or the background of the Europe he knew.

But it was the chimpanzee's fate which caught my attention in reading about Mühsam's life--not the others, for their story has been told. Being a lover of Leviathan, had it not been for the fate of this animal which joined Mühsam's fate, I would not have written my story, for politically and socially, philosophically I have little in common with these prisoners, certainly not with Mühsam, nor any desire to emulate Jesus, certainly not his manner of dying. Being a citizen of the world--a townswoman--more like Zensl, needing to be comforted and prepared, I have no politics--at least, no good politics, only loyalties. As a writer, I

am not fond of café literature, protest literature, of proclamations in the street. I believe in discipline and silence--the silence of anger. Least of all do I believe in applause, or an audience, or even attention. It is dangerous--attention. Angels in the guise of writers should move invisibly and silently--sshh

#

Father Woytzski Leads A Jewish Youth Group To The Holocaust Memorial In Oswiecim, Poland

He began this work eighteen years after the war had ended and he had been liberated from Auschwitz. Nothing in his previous life, not even his internment in the camp, had prepared him for this kind of work; but then nothing in his life, or anyone else's that he knew of, had prepared him for the camp, for his flight, not prompted by political motives, from his native country, a rural village in the Malapolska Hills between Lodz and Cracow; nor for his subsequent life in a lower middle class neighborhood in Brooklyn, a neighborhood without hills and few trees, with many schoolyards and playgrounds which he passed daily on his walk from St. Stephen's Parish to the multitudinous meetings that fill the time of a clergyman.

From meeting to meeting, he passed through these Jewish neighborhoods, the schoolyards crowded with children swinging bats and books, the girls on bicycles, already flirting, already recovering: the children of the next generation, the generation of the sons of Noah, born after the flood. Though he had been in Auschwitz with their parents, he never tarried here. His life of recovery had its own pattern. The war had caused disruptions in many lives, but it had shattered his differently. A more than ordinary sense of discontinuity haunted him so that he seemed not to have spiritual autonomy any longer.

Since his internment at Auschwitz he suffered from this lack of "spiritual familiarity," and was prone to dreams and experiences that were inexplicable to him which, as he described them, seized him "with an outside force," explicable perhaps in someone else's life but not in his; for he was temperamentally a moderate man, of middle height, well read in Plotinus and Patristic literature, and not given to a Gothic sensibility.

Nevertheless, these experiences arrived in due course. And for all their regularity, occurring every three or four months, weakened him for days. They were like "an attack," or a "fit" of illness, something one had to recover from. Which he always did, though they left a residue of anxiety, layer upon layer, after each attack. The last experience had occurred in his own church while he was performing Mass: the feeling that Christ had descended from the crucifix behind him, not to embrace him, but to assault him.

He recognized the aberration as one of many he had had over the years, and forced himself to continue with the Mass. He refused to allow "private" experiences to expel him from his traditions, from his framework of reality. He was unprepared for a radical departure, for his own saintliness.

The first experience had occurred upon his release from Auschwitz. Before his internment he had been a village priest in a farming district, when he had been seized and taken prisoner: he was not sympathetic to Jews. In fact, there in the Malapolska Hills where he had been born, the problem was remote, a theological problem one read about in the Gospels, or a political problem one read about in the newspapers. If they were the People of the Book they were also the people in the Book. Like everyone else in the farming district he lived in, he had seen Jews on the few occasions he had gone to Lodz or Cracow where they were for him disembodied figures in the modern structure.

Then one night a Jewish woman materialized out of nowhere at the door of his house in the village somewhere between Lodz and Cracow, materialized out of the night and the impact of history, banging loudly on his door. His terrified housekeeper refused to answer the knock. He went himself, prepared to confront police, German soldiers, people with helmets, guns! For what? He had done nothing, was guilty of nothing. This innocence gave him the assurance that whoever was knocking on his door had come to the wrong place, and he opened the door. A woman, about his own age, unkempt and bleeding for some reason, a frantic, brawling child in her arms, collapsed into his room. Immediately he put up his hands, forewarned and asked her not to reveal her identity, and said to his housekeeper, "It's only a woman with a hungry child. Make something to eat."

The child--about two, he surmised, and rather a good size to carry a distance--was so frantic, it could not swallow. His hunger had made him self destructive. They had to hold his arms down and force the food into him. The woman sat at the table and ate, and called his name (Pietzka) between mouthfuls, and begged him to be good and eat, "for you see," she wept,"these people are kind."

Little by little the child's screaming stopped. When he was finally at peace, the housekeeper, watching from the doorway, relaxed from her tension. For at all times and everywhere it is unbearable to listen to a hungry child. They hurriedly dressed the woman's wounds, conversed minimally, gave her bread to take with her and she departed, her child strapped to her back.

They stood in the dining room, he and his housekeeper, and looked at each other. She spoke first. "Well, that's that."

Two days later he was accused of giving refuge to a Jew and his church was ordered closed. He explained that he had no idea who the woman was, but that he would comply with their orders. From week to week, from Sunday to Sunday, from Mass to Mass, he intended to comply. Until they came one morning on motorcycles, helmeted. His arms, raised with the host, remained in midair, paralyzed with terror (they described it as "intractable rebelliousness"). They tore the Crucifix from its place, dismantled the altar with an ax, and marched him into a car, into a prison, into an office where he was interrogated, into another prison where he was tortured, and into Auschwitz where he was interned.

He emerged two years later, very old, and went back to his village, to his church, out of habit: every familiar stone, every bit of color from the windows anticipated with hunger.

But someone had replaced the Crucifix. To his surprise, he noted this with resentment. He had come to replace it himself. Someone had disturbed the sequence of events, his place in the restoration of order. A rebelliousness broke out in his mind: "We can no longer say that Your death was quintessential in its suffering. Calvary is everywhere." The thought--so unprepared he was to have it--seemed to demand that he leave the priesthood. One for whom distant events were no further away than yesterday, Calvary as omnipresent as Auschwitz, this meditation seemed inexcusable.

It was the nature of his temperament that he rose from his bench in the church, prepared to follow the dictates of this argument and leave the priesthood. He slept that night in the village inn and there began those dreams of the Crucifix that were to follow him the rest of his life. The figure spoke to him with presumptuous candor, a message he was doomed to hear. This dream, as most dreams with a message, was imperative, but he could not understand it. Upon waking, he was acutely uncomfortable to realize that in his dream he had prayed that he never would understand it. There began that feeling of hiatus, of a split in his personality, of being borne whither he would not go, of being seized by a spiritual current whose direction he distrusted, of being the unwilling carrier of a message he prayed not to hear.

Within the next few days he made up his mind to leave Europe, to cut loose from this past which had become disorganized in his mind so that he was rapidly losing the historical sense of it, without which he could have no theology.

In the aftermath of the war, such feelings came too rapidly and violently for him to digest. In the face of so much disintegration he could hope only to save himself and not his priesthood, and so came to the United States with the thousands of other refugees in that time. He remained a priest, for practical reasons only. It placed him quickly, occupationally, and severed bureaucratic knots. Officials were assured he was not a "displaced person." These gratuitous assumptions fed his sense of shame. He sat huddled in a deck chair on the boat, remorseful that he was granted a "saving faith."

Many Jews were on the boat with him. He recognized a few as having been in his camp, but he felt no desire to talk with them. Almost everyone stood at the rail and watched the ocean beneath them or the horizon ahead of them. Subject to perverse moods, he thought: "These are the generations of Isaac---why do they always suffer such ludicrous fates?" unmindful of the fact that he shared this one with them. He felt no grudge against the woman whose life he had saved and bestowed upon the incident no further sentiment. "They had been caught off guard." "They had acted instinctively, out of mere human charity." "Even animals do as much." Statements he had made in defense of himself, but when asked to denounce his "regrettable error," silence had afflicted him.

Neither did the rolling ocean or the blue sky or the first seagull, when it was sighted and faces lifted towards it and eyes fluttered at it, neither did these call him out to life. He sensed no future for himself.

A Jew stopped in front of his chair, his shirtsleeves rolled up, his number apparent on his hairy arm. "So," he said, "so now we know. Before Hitler God was helpless, Christ was helpless. Even the Pope was helpless. Now, what?"

Father Woytzski shielded his eyes from the amazing sun. He was surprised, again, by his emotions. A pugilistic reflex to defend himself made him say, "You resent Christianity? Christ?"

The Jew clasped his hands behind his back: a philosophical pose. What had he been before the war? A professor, a lawyer, a tailor? Impossible to know in the nondescript refugee clothes he wore. "He's not Christ," he said. Father Woytzski dropped his arm. The man shimmered in the sunlight. "He's not Meshiach. When Meshiach comes, he won't fail."

Father Woytzski was greedy for the sun. This man cast a shadow on his face. "You'll never change," he said to him.

"What's to change?" the man said, "me or the world?"

"They'll burn you again."

The obscenity bounced off him. "Me they didn't get, and even if they did still wouldn't make 1+ 1=3. Akiba was wrong and so was Jesus. We saw right away he was wrong. And that other one, Sabbatai Zevi. We saw he was wrong too."

Father Woytzski put his arm over his eyes. In spite of the man's shadow they were tearing from the light. "Why do you deny Christ?"

The man snorted. "Who has a better right? I'm the opposition. But you? What's your reason?"

A sibilant sound went up from the boat, sigh or moan: land was sighted. He took his arm away from his eyes. All the faces at the rail were indistinguishable, all eyes were in one direction. No one stood in front of him.

Father Woytzski did not leave the priesthood. He suffered it. He undertook it as the cross he no longer believed in, "the burden of his atheism," and paid the price of self reproach and of the world as shadow. He committed no transgressions, for nothing tempted him. He suffered sleeplessness and loss of appetite in everything, even for intellectual activity. Messages of his coming crisis reached him from within: the troubled dreams, the "aberrations," the inexplicable sensations that someone waited for him behind closed doors, that someone had a message for him; and always waking at dawn, someone coughing surreptitiously, coughing behind his hand, getting up the sputum with an effort. Father Woytzski hated the sound of it, with its memories of sickbeds, urinals and latrines, the smells of bodily decay eating away at his faith in immortality: history and theology reduced to the problem of fecal matter. "Go away," he groaned. The man obliged. He rolled off the edge of the bed and rocked on his heels, broken with hunger and spite.

The fool would rock forever if someone didn't stop him! Someone stopped him. The next night it was quiet and Father Woytzski slept through. Five, six, seven nights until the coughing woke him again. Eventually, it always did. And he always had the same response. Enough! "Damn you, go away!"

This nocturnal argument continued for years. His nights acquired a shadow history, a dialogue without language, so old that gestures sufficed. This argument between himself and his "opposition" was immemorial (he could not remember when it had begun), and irremediable (would not yield to the intellect). They wrestled, he and his "opposition," this specter of resistance clinging to life, coughing up sputum, wiping the saliva from its lips. Extraordinary for European history to have taken this pathetic form. Only he seemed aware of this, "visited" with this chilling information. In the daytime, he ignored it. In the daytime he followed the same course from meeting to meeting, Sunday to Sunday, Mass to Mass. Though he wrote many articles for religious newspapers and journals, he never discussed this problem in them. He believed that his personal fears had no place in the daytime world of dialogue.

But at night it was otherwise. He was transformed into a morbid consciousness, a register of antinomians. The idea that "nothing makes sense," neither Jesus' divinity nor the Jews' rejection of him, could be understood philosophically. He required a reconciliation which would allow him his faith. The Father, the Son, and the Holy Ghost co-eternal, and in contradiction of the first commandment: a jealous God debased by the coming of the Son whom Father Woytzski's faith glorified: debased and glorified their God, their Father the devil who so loved the world He gave His only begotten son. To what conclusion had the centuries brought him: to the conclusion that none of it made sense: easy enough to say if you're not looking for God; difficult to shake the terror of it if you are.

"Enough!" he called out. But to whom did he address these words. At the end of his bed was nothing but the cluttered gatherings of his blanket where his feet had pushed it. The figure continued to cough and to wipe the prayer in his mouth with his shawl, the blanket on his bed. History and personal memory conspired. God knows the number of Jews he might have seen like this in his camp. But now he could not remember if he had ever seen a Jew in such a posture, or was constructing his memory from photographs he had seen. He both remembered and didn't remember. History and memory lost their boundaries, became each other, the past and his present. The boundaries of his psyche became fluid. At night, more and more often, he could not remember what century he belonged to, and wondered if it made a difference. Fear told him it did. Fear told him to cling to the mortality he knew was his own, to stay in his own flesh and to die in it, above all, above all, to stay in his own flesh, to cling to the century he was born to and vindicate it.

The figure at the end of his bed rose, as he remembered it doing a few minutes ago, rose and rocked on its feet in prayer, as he knew it would, for whatever reason he knew this. A conspiracy of shadows attacked him, a merging of dream intentions, an everlasting Protean wickedness of night stuff: The Lord shall smite thee with madness and with astonishment of heart!

No one can account for the deepest springs in another, for what is called simply "a change of heart," or melodramatically "a conversion." Here comes one who halts one day in front of the schoolyard of a yeshiva. An action arrested Father Woytzski's attention. A boy of eleven, yarmulka on head, cracked a bat, hit a two base run and took off. Cap on head hit the wind and flew off. The retrieval was instinctive, and the batter was knocked out by the infielder. His disappointment, always plain on the faces of the young, arrested Father Woytzski's attention. He had a generous impulse to tell the boy that it was not his fault--if he hadn't bent to retrieve his cap--that you mustn't be distracted from the game. He walked away, amazed by his thoughts. A perilous irony hung over them.

That night he dreamed that he was back in his village, in his church, in his own church in the Malapolska

Hills, and that he had come to restore the Crucifix to its rightful place, for no one had. He had been mistaken in that. He woke and prepared himself, as a Jew, to read the Bible, and discovered that he could not. Incoherence rose from the familiar pages.

Throughout the years, Father Woytzski dreamed of many things that bore resemblance to the dreams of others: of being pursued, being buried in pits, in holes, in wells, all suspect of Freudian meanings; being buried in impossible situations, "implacably totalitarian," as Poe intended in "The Pit and the Pendulum" where a man searches for means of escape from the conditions of world and history by means of the rational self. But upon waking, he always knew that he had dreamed of Auschwitz, for prior to his imprisonment when he was a village priest and a young man, he dreamed very different dreams: he dreamed he was being pursued, buried in pits and in caves, in holes and in wells, but he was always rescued, mysteriously and sweetly rescued, justifying faith in God and the world.

Now, waking in the middle of the night, he would turn on his light and reach for his Gospel. Then he would remember the shadow in his dream that was empty of content, that had no salvation, no rescue, no marvelous deus ex machina, the saving hand of dreamers.

In the morning on the way to a hospital or a visit to someone's home, he passed the yeshiva schoolyard crowded with school buses and children. Quaint! Quaint! All this restoration! These pushing, shoving children waiting for doors to open, their voices already hoarse with morning prayers and jibes at each other, mothers waving their goodbyes, as if none of it had happened. Babies in their

arms, babies by the hand. Quaint! He shared a nightlife with them, a nocturnal dialogue, but in the daytime their alliance was rhetorical. Quaint! He dreamed about them every night. The quaintness of it struck him again. A cold calamity sprang from the ground. There, on the brink of spring, the trees stiff with buds, the air hovering with green, in the shouting of their optimistic voices, cold calamity sprang from the ground. Everything hung in the balance: air and sun and bird pinned against the sky, and his soul wrestling for recovery.

He dreamed that night, again, of his church in the Malapolska Hills. He entered and found the Crucifix where it had fallen, and bent to pick it up, but was prevented by his weeping. He could not pick it up. He could do nothing but weep at where it had fallen. When he woke, he did not feel guilty that he had failed. But neither could he remember whether he had gone back to his church after leaving Auschwitz. He had only the impression of having done so, not even a memory anymore. But, surely he had gone back! Why else had he left Poland? Because he had gone back--and had seen what? What had he seen that would have caused him to leave? Memory, so dependent upon the personal self, wavered. The boundary between events became more obscure; his crisis deepened.

He sought avenues of "religious rehabilitation": ecumenical councils, neighborhood interfaith discussions. He encouraged his parishioners to attend a seder on Passover night. He initiated interfaith prayers on Thanksgiving evening. But these did not give him peace. His dream life continued until it began to usurp his waking life and to exhaust it. The liaisons he assiduously promoted felt too fragile, too contemporary, perhaps too American, to withstand the pressure of the past. Everything hung in the balance.

Beset with fears about his "true feelings" on this matter, nevertheless, one year he accepted Rabbi Zellenberg's proposal to accompany him and a dozen children to Dachau. His work in the community and his feelings on these matters were respected. He, himself, had been in Auschwitz. He had the credentials of Lazarus. The invitation stirred his uneasiness about the world's gratuitous assumption about his "saving faith."

That first trip--he was to take half a dozen with Rabbi Zellenberg--was fraught with his self consciousness as the "expert," the "survivor" among these children who sat on the plane, intensely sober and frozen lipped. Rabbi Zellenberg was nervous and kept setting the yarmulkas straight on the boys' heads. Weary, he finally fell asleep next to Chaim, his "star pupil," the one who would vindicate him as a teacher. As they sighted the coastline of Europe, three children began to sing Hatikvah in thin voices. Then they landed, and filed off the airplane behind Rabbi Zellenberg, prepared to meet their nightmare with a few rituals and prayers.

Still, Father Woytzski went the next year and the year after that. Rabbi Zellenberg became "the expert," and Father Woytzski left the discipline of the children and the singing to him. Each year brought changes. The trauma acquired specificity; the boundary between black and not-so-black determined the discriminating details so necessary for the register of reality and survival. The forces of good and evil became clarified, lifted from the anarchy of mystery and nightmare; and their singing became stronger, their repertoire of songs fuller.

Each year brought its own embarrassments, differences, limits, constraints, revelations. Each year he felt himself traveling in altogether different directions, further back, further apart from the others, for the children changed from year to year. An appetite for knowing colored the sobriety of the first trip. Afterwards, they were inevitably more sophisticated, mastering the wave, putting distance between themselves and this past, taking their measure of life against this shadow; except for himself who seemed to be traveling elsewhere, into a knowledge which he wished not to master.

Then Rabbi Zellenberg took ill and died. It was the year they planned to go to Auschwitz. Father Woytzski's position as a native of Poland, as a former inmate of Auschwitz, one who was not Jewish, one who was a priest, helped persuade the Polish officials. But other than Peter Zelkin, age twenty, member of the Youth Council of the temple, no other adult accompanied him. The new rabbi, Rabbi Scheller's wife was expecting their first baby. Father Woytzski went himself, with twelve children. He it was who had to address the Brotherhood on financial matters, he it was who received calls from anxious parents, advice as to allergies, food problems, homesickness, letter writing. He it was who went to visit them to discuss that which fell into the category of "special problems." He preached a sermon the Sunday before he left on "the True Sepulchre of Christ, for Auschwitz," he said, "and "not Calvary had been omnipresent these forty years."

The weeks prior to his leaving were filled with the flurry of activity that used to fall to the responsibility of

Rabbi Zellenberg. It was Father Woytzski who arrived at Mrs. Rosenbloom's house, cluttered with the treasured photographs of weddings and babies, trays of candlesticks, silver and brass and glass, and wall hangings of Sfad, the Galilee, and Jerusalem the Golden. Her mother-in-law, a stubborn babushka on her head, followed after them with scruffy footsteps, after her grandchildren, Danny, aged twelve, and Sharon, aged fifteen, "the special problem."

They sat in the living room and discussed Sharon, budding in a T shirt which girls now wore, some with alarming messages written on them. Disingenuously, hers read, "I'm Heaven Sent and Earthward Bound."

"Sharon needs watching," Mrs. Rosenbloom said.

The old lady sat at the window and "watched the outside." She grunted her disagreement.

Mrs. Rosenbloom did not say anything more. She wished only to hint and to find herself at the conclusion of the conversation, without using words to get there. She wished Father Woytzski to understand without her having to explain anything. She got little further than "things" would have been easier if Rabbi Zellenberg had not died." He had known Sharon since she was born. However, they had promised her this trip this year and they could not go back on their word. She pushed tea and cake at him. He accepted and pondered her message. The old lady continued to sit at the window, seemingly excluded from tea and cake and comment. Danny added, "I've read Shirer."

"In school?" Father Woytzski asked.

"Are you kidding?" he sneered, "they don't teachya anything in school."

A month later, Danny arrived at the airport, Shirer in hand, Sharon in a blue T shirt that read, "I Get Better on Acquaintance." Twenty-four parents, eight grandmothers, three grandfathers, and twelve children assembled. Rabbi Scheller conducted a prayer service in the waiting room for the safe return of the travelers. A thousand "Be good's," "Be careful's," and they were boarding. But not before the old lady pushed her way through the crowd on shuffling feet to Father Woytzski, babushka on head, yellow teeth hissing in his native Polish, the dialect of his hills, "Go with God, I'll pray for you. My prayers are special. Go."

They boarded: to fly to Warsaw, to visit Lodz, to take the bus to his village in the Malapolska Hills, to take the train to Cracow, to take the bus from there to Oswiecim. Through the whole of the trip Sharon's wardrobe consisted of two pairs of Levis, one dress (for shul) and T-shirts in assorted colors and assorted messages for the Polish world: "To Know Me Is To Love Me."

In Warsaw she sat on the bus and two boys, flaxen-haired and blue-eyed, made out the message and sat down in front of her. Danny jabbed her in her ribs with his elbow, and went back to his reading. Her shirts caused stares and comments wherever she went: On Monday, "Try Me." On Tuesday, "To Know Me Is To Want Me,' on Wednesday, "Too Hot to Handle." On Thursday--Father Woytzski averted his eyes.

He wondered that her parents allowed her to pack such shirts. But then, all the girls in America now wore them with a curious innocence. Even the girls in the schoolyard of St. Stephen's school. No one else in the group noticed, not even Peter Zelkin. Peter himself wore a shirt which froze Father Woytzski's blood. Black on grey, it read, "I Explode On Contact." Sharon seemed not to notice the attention she caused, or did not wish for the others to know that she noticed. She stared out the window of the bus at the streets of Warsaw, the disarming bearer of a message to the flaxen-haired and the blue-eyed. She was, no more and no less, a child of her generation, the children of the sons of Noah who had floated on the waters of destruction.

They spent three days in Warsaw, one day at the site of the ghetto, walking around it, walking through it, huddled in its museum. In their dungarees and T shirts, in the freedom of this fashion, they seemed fragile and unprotected.

On the fourth day, they took a bus to Lodz. It was crowded with other passengers, other young boys in Levis and leather jackets who themselves seemed transformed into American figures: brisk movements, good spirits, curiosity about these Americans, self conscious, defensive, arrogant, good humored. Father Woytzski's clerical garb and Polish past were a bridge. They asked questions. He explained "the pilgrimage." They knew something about it. They asked him about America, many questions about America. They asked him what was written on the shirts. Father Woytzski forebore. "Sayings," he said. One winked and said he could read a little English. He read the message on Sharon's shirt. They laughed. They were intrigued. American girls were always so interesting. They pushed to sit down in front of her. Sharon kept her face out the window. Danny jabbed her again in her ribs and said, "Now see what you've done!" Sharon jabbed back. "I haven't done anything." Danny knew this was so, but that was not enough to appease him. He jabbed her back. "Yes, you have," he whispered. Sharon suffered the ugliness of being accused unjustly. Her blue eyes leaped to the fight. The two boys in front of her had no idea what caused the flare-up in her eyes, but they were intrigued. "What is your name?" one asked in Polish.

She did not understand. He tried the sentence in English. "Your name? What is?"

"Sharon."

"Sharon? What means Sharon?"

It was time to intervene. They were not far from Lodz. Father Woytzski directed their attention to the view outside, though he himself regarded it with armored distance, testing his thirty-five years of residence in the United States against it. They--the American group--and the four Polish boys--parted in Lodz. They--the American group spent two days in Lodz, circling the ghetto there, that unique European creation, a "neighborhood" with names like Judenstrasse and Judenplatz, which had breathed its affects into so many aspects of European life, its restrictions a curiosity for American children who at age ten know how to cut a hole in a hurricane fence with a pair of pliers and enter any playground at will. Nevertheless, this is their past. Though they do not remember the flood, they know that it happened and move through its neighborhood accordingly.

Then they boarded the bus again, this time for Father Woytzski's village in the Malapolska Hills, prepared as they had agreed to do, to go all the way back with him, to see the village where he had been born, the school where he had been educated, the house he had lived in, for whatever he had become to them in their Jewish neighborhood in Brooklyn, here is where he began. And they were prepared to do him this honor.

They boarded the bus and struck for the hills, not only for the cities with its defined circumferences and its life labelled with street signs where you can find your way around with civic accommodations--but for the open country where change is slow and freedom is only apparent, where old religions, as the Christians discovered among the rural pagans of Gaul, take a long time to die. It was here, in one of these small villages, that six Jews had returned from Auschwitz to collect their belongings, and were murdered by the villagers. "Lynched," as they say in the United States.

Father Woytzski suddenly felt nervous, confronted by memories which brought him into judgment upon his own people. But the consequences of this trip took another turn, though given the quixotic nature of a tradition, even the religious tradition, it could just as well have taken the earlier fate. Traditions are like Greek masks and can slip from one expression to the other with a sleight of hand. In this case it wore the expression of geniality.

Two of the boys--the ones with the flaxen hair and the blue eyes--in Levis and leather jackets, boarded the bus at Lodz. They too were going all the way through to Cracow. They too were stopping off in the Malapolska Hills. They had a grandmother who lived there, an uncle in Lodz, a sister in Cracow. This was their holiday. They were visiting everyone. They were traveling through Poland. Some day they hoped to come to the United States. They were very interested in this American group, also touring Poland, yarmulkas discounted. In America, things were different. If they could come to America, they were prepared to be different too. They slipped into the seat behind Sharon and Danny and engaged them in conversation. They wished to engage Sharon, but Danny was the informed one. He happened to have an almanac in his pocket. They listened politely, learned very little, and kept their eyes on Sharon. Soon they were in heat and it made them silly. They giggled a lot and became very friendly. They flashed their stunning hair in her eyes. They became ardent supporters of anything she might want. They could show her a lot in the village.

The American group practiced indifference. Flirting they understood (except for Danny) but history warned them against it here. But Sharon was not indifferent. She was embarrassed but excited. Father Woytzski intervened again. His tactic was to distract with loftier conversation. Of course it didn't work. They with the flaxen hair answered him perfunctorily, and went back to paying attention to Sharon. Danny's method was more direct. He jabbed Sharon in her ribs again. She turned her pent-up emotions on him and began to pummel him. At once, this made her more appealing. Nothing now could prevail against their ardor.

Seeing that levity didn't work, they too became serious. They discussed Poland's offenses against the Jews which they attributed to economic malaise, the innumerable invasions by Germany and Russia, medieval superstitions, and an impoverished peasantry. But now with economic reform, all was different. They were different. They swung their hair.

Sharon gave way. She said she had nothing against the Polish people. (They were very glad to hear this.) In America all ethnic groups were equal. Polish people had the same rights as everyone else, Jews and Germans and Blacks.

They listened with respect: America was a wonderful country.

The bus arrived in the late afternoon on this agreeable note. The depot was the parking lot behind the village hotel. They got off, shaking hands with everyone; with Father Woytzski, whom they now treated with more respect, with Peter Zelkin, whose T shirt and yarmulkah seemed unstably mixed, with Danny who quoted Orwell's aphorisms to them, and with Sharon, whose hand they held longer than the others. Could they come and visit her this evening? Their grandmother's house was only a block away. They would love for their grandmother to meet her, to meet them.

Father Woytzski thought not, and felt the peculiarity of his reservations. What grounds did he have for objecting? they wanted to know. In America, everyone was equal. Was this not so? They were puzzled. They wished to place the hospitality of their village, their country, at his disposal. Their grandmother baked wonderful breads, always ready in the oven.

Peter told Father Woytzski to accept the offer but he looked about at the village, its two or three dozen houses, the dusty road, the hills in the retreating background, straightened his yarmulkah on his head, folded his arms on his chest, and kicked the tire of the bus.

Sharon felt required to attack his churlishness. The terms of her American upbringing seemed to her to require this. "They're only being polite," she said. She went further. After washing up and when they came down to the dining room, she said that she was humiliated by the way they behaved. Peter's kicking the tire of the bus was like kicking them in the face--for what?--"for inviting us to meet their grandmother?" Peter denied nothing and added nothing.

Father Woytzski saw himself as the cause of Peter's constraint, the motive for Sharon's defense, though what he had wished for most ardently was not to be the pertinent factor in their behavior.

The two brothers came at dusk in high spirits, still in Levis and leather jackets in spite of the twilight warmth. Their grandmother was expecting them, they said, particularly Father Woytzski. She was beside herself with surprise and joy when she heard that he had returned. The brothers beamed their message. They looked at Father Woytzski with more vigorous respect. Would he remember his old housekeeper? He was startled. "She must be over a hundred." "Yes," the brothers said, "but wonderfully strong."

The group walked down the dusty street behind Father Woytzski and Peter, his arms folded on his chest, the two boys with the flaxen hair on either side of Sharon, outdoing each other in garrulity. "Their grandmother's bread was wonderful." "How wonderful that she should be Father Woytzski's old housekeeper." "What a wonderful homecoming for him." "American girls were wonderful." "Could they maybe write to her." "Maybe someday they could come to America and see her." "Could they have her address?"

Their grandmother was already in the doorway, watching for them. She could not believe that Father Woytzski had returned. He had disappeared after the war. Everyone thought he had died in Auschwitz. A miracle had happened. She gathered him up as if his true place had been restored to him. Her joy, so genuine, embraced only him. He introduced the children to her but her eyes, filled with the miracle of his return, swept over them casually. What had America made of him? He thought that his appearance there with this group explained it. Her grandsons explained to her in Polish, the object of their trip. She brushed their explanation aside as if they had said something naughty and it wasn't worth her while to discipline them for it. What mattered was that Father Woytzski had returned. He had not forgotten his birthplace. All these years she had been praying for his soul in heaven, and he had been in America.

After the visit, the group returned to the inn, not really a group any longer. In Warsaw, in Lodz, they recognized their history. Here, in this village, among the eternal hills, it was different. They had come with a different set of rules about ethnic parity and "not excluding people." The old woman had ignored their rules. She ignored America. Here everything was the same as it had been. No America.

"Well, you can see why she ignored us," Sharon said. "After all, she was his housekeeper. Naturally, she wanted to spend all her time talking with him." The others were not persuaded. Their spirits sagged. They looked forward to leaving the village.

To his surprise, Father Woytzski was dismayed by Sharon's defense. He was pleased to see his old housekeeper,

but the feeling was guarded by the sense that the bridge between them had collapsed. She only imagined that he was back, and it had embarrassed him, again, to be the recipient of religious goodwill. On the other hand, he had an impulse to shake Sharon from her American armor, but the sense that he had no rights over her stopped the words that came to his lips. He only said, mildly enough, "Oh, child, really!" But that was wound enough to her. She went upstairs to her room, conspicuously insulted.

Father Woytzski retired with unpleasant reflections. He wanted above all not to dissipate the spirit of the group, not to be the instrument of its loss of momentum. Not recompense, but recovery was possible, was on the wing, and he wanted to be part of it and not dissipate its energy. It had not been pleasant for him to realize that in his old housekeeper's mind, nothing had changed, not even him. She was a difficult yardstick, that old lady. She was his old human attachments, his womb of memory.

He planned to visit his old church in the morning, but he was beset with hesitation, with a feeling that he had not earned the right to go back, because the return, so longed for humanly, now seemed to bargain on the sanctity of the children in his charge. The feeling of hiatus occurred in him again. It was not as sharp as it used to be. He did not have the sensation that he was being literally torn apart. His energies were not consumed in protecting himself, and now he remembered when he had first felt it. It was when that woman had knocked on his door and he had responded instinctively, like an animal leaping to the defense of its own: life calling to life through the chaos of history.

A dusky moon hung in the sky, his sky, the moon of warm summer nights in rural places that brought such richness to a country night. He could not forget it nor account for how he had squandered it. Had he not convinced himself, here, many years ago, of the beneficence of life. It had been his own youth which had convinced him of it. Yet a chill struck him. The richness of the moon was pregnant with premonition. He put on his bathrobe and slippers and went down the stairs to the small lobby. There were whispers in the doorway. Two blonde heads bobbed in the moonlight. Father Woytzski felt a wrath invade his bones. "Sharon," he called sharply. There was a muted exclamation, and she fled. "Go away," he said to the blonde heads. "We came only to say goodbye," they said affably. "Go away," he said again. They did, but not without mumbling about his sourness. Sharon waited for him at the top of the steps, still in her dungarees and T shirt. "How could you!" she said in a shrill voice, wounded in the marrow of her womanhood.

He went back to his room and lay down, a prey to introspection. He took himself to task for over-reacting. He went over it a dozen times, but each time became more convinced that she was wrong and he was right. He was right to have been indignant, even if she was a child. How else should one react to a foolish child? Oh! child, child. How many hearts have burst for you? He could not sleep anymore. He must walk off his thoughts. Again, he put on his bathrobe and his slippers and went down the steps. He should have gone first to the church and not delayed to see if the Crucifix had been restored. That should have been the first thing he should have done. He hurried there now. In the moonlight of these streets, all the skeins of this history shone twisted and braided. Child! Child! he mumbled as he ran, overwhelmed with the everlastingness of her fallible humanity: Even the generations of the sons of Noah, the ones who came after the flood.

The door was open, waiting for him. The pews and the benches were in order. The Crucifix was in its place, over his old altar. The moonlight came in through the open door and the windows, washing over the ivory body, lighting the carved face. The eyes gleamed at him. The message stared from them. How hard it was to accept it. Oh, fallible humanity! How awesome was this fallible humanity! Whose heart could stand it? Whose heart could die for it? "Take me instead," Moses had said. "If Thou must blot out this people, take me instead." Oh, treasure of caring which had never ceased. "I have come to save the House of Israel." Oh, heart! Oh, terrible failure! Oh, terrible heartbreak of history.

His knees bent under the weight of this revelation into the wounded heart of his Saviour, the pathos of this history. It was his own heart that broke, his own tears that fell.

#

The Enigmatic Power of the Letter "J"

The Mapuche believe that the history of the world is inscribed on everyone's body, like the rings in a tree. Therefore the "J" in the middle of Estrellita's forehead could not be erased by a doctor or the medicine woman. Her mother hid the mark as best she could by cutting Estrellita's hair with a deep fringe to cover it. But everyone knew what was beneath the fringe. When Estrellita was alone she would lift up her bangs and look at the letter that had been branded into her forehead, hoping that it would not be there, that her face would be the one she knew before this had happened to her, but a stranger had put his stamp on her face and had made her his. Her face no longer belonged to her and her soul was no longer hers.

Her parents gasped when they saw her in the hospital. Their expressions went into Estrellita's heart like a knife, but they did not explain why this had been done to her. No one could explain what the sign meant. The medicine woman could say nothing about it, and she could not make it disappear. Its power was stronger than hers. The villagers said Estrellita had become a kaluka, a spirit which causes mischief and ill will and they would have nothing to do with her anymore.

Everyone in the fishing village, a spit of land between forest and mountains saved from the ocean, knew within a day after she had been rescued what had happened to her, and everyone had an interpretation. The Indians applied their theory of accounting for evil done to a person: It would not be done by kin who knew her and would not do this, or by strangers who did not know her and therefore had no reason to do this; the evil therefore must have been done by proximate strangers who bore her ill will. Estrellita said she had seen her assailants and they had white faces. Neither was this a good interpretation, for the villagers did not wish to have the government descend upon them to investigate. It was better to believe that Estrellita had been selected by the god who lives in volcanoes and consorts with the evil that roams the earth. The volcanoes gossip constantly with tongues of fire about such evils, about danger and change; never about comfort and safety. They are always on the verge of erupting and changing the landscape. Ice floes come down from Patagonia bearing stranded penguins who gaze at their change in location with quizzical patience. It is a difficult landscape, full of tongues made of fire and ice.

The sons of hidalgos, the "Chileans," who own the terraced farms and sheep ranches above the village believed Indians had done this. Mapuches like her father came every spring from the island of Chiloé to work for them. He himself had worked like this for three seasons, and then left the reservation on Chiloé to become a fisherman with sails and nets with his mark woven into them. He sold his fish in Osorno, where they fetched high prices in the German beer halls.

Estrellita or her brothers sometimes went out with him in his rowboat when his working day was over. She loved to feel the waves pass through her fingers trailing in the water. But at this time her father stayed near the shore because at sunset the souls of the dead are carried out into the West, scooped into the hand of the sunset and carried out to where the silver steamers split the horizon in two. Those ships came from where Estrellita's mother's ancestors had come from centuries ago. The sea had brought them into the village where they had married mestizos and Mapuche, and came to look like them except that they did not eat pork. The villagers were sometimes unkind about things like this and Estrellita's brothers, being men, snapped their fingers at the village and left. Every evening, out there where the land split off from the heavens and the night swallowed the sun, there was a struggle between good and evil, between darkness and light. The only mercy Ngenenchen, the Creator, showed to humans was to close up the future so that no one could know his hour of death. That was Ngenenchen's mercy: to close up the future.

Sometimes Estrellita and her brothers went with their father in his truck to Osorno to sell his fish. Though the grocers called them "cholitos" and beckoned them to drop their coins into their palms so that they would not have to touch their fingers, they could not resist the markets and bought sausages, strudel, and tortes with layers of chocolate and raspberry. Music bands played polkas in the beer halls and military bands played in the parks. Soldiers paraded in the streets with German flags with swastikas on them, while boatloads of immigrants disembarked to find that this remote city was a small Europe, and they were face to face with the same enemy.

Her mother never went to Osorno. After her sons left for Santiago, they pleaded with her to live with one of them, but her refusal to go anywhere was adamant. Here she had nailed up bark from the canelo pine over her doorway to keep away evil spirits the way her ancestors had nailed up olive wood over doorways in Spain with prayers transcribed in them. A bargain had been struck with the gods of survival, and she believed it was her fate to stay here.

Her tenacity surprised them, for they knew her as a girlish old woman. The stubborness of the aged is a mystery to the young, and her sons were furious with her, like children are with a parent they want to save, who has become intractable. Whenever they came to visit, which became less and less frequent, their quarrels were bitter. They would go away and swear never to come back. "What for? What do you have here? Look what they did to Estrellita. Do you want to stay here until they murder her?"

Their bitterness and their love wrestled like Siamese twins that could not be parted and could not live together. Bonded hip to hip and thigh to thigh, they smote each others' faces. At least Estrellita should go, they said, but she would not go either, because she believed the rest of the world was populated by white people who had turned her into a kaluka. She had seen the faces of her assailants by the firelight. They were round and white, their hair was yellow and their breath smelled hot with beer. They were the faces she saw in Osorno, and she could not go there anymore. Since her abduction a shadow covered her eyes which drained everything of color. She could not see things as she once had. Her eyes had been stolen from her and a different pair of eyes had been put into her head, which made everything look gray. She stumbled about and tried to find the world she had once known. Then a noise, the sound of a car or waves rattled the nightmare in her head and the world jumped out at her from a hiding place. She could not see what she wanted to see, the world she had once known, and she could not stop seeing what she did not want to see: boys with yellow moon heads on a March evening who had dragged her into their car when she walked home from a store. They dragged her into a cave on the beach and tied her hands and feet. The cheese she had bought fell from her hands. The boys built a fire and opened cans of beer. They knew what they were going to do with Estrellita, but could not decide who should do it. They tied her ankles and her wrists and drank the beer while they discussed what they were going to do. Then they drew lots. The boy who won, or lost, picked up the branding iron with the letter "J" on it that they had stolen from a sheep ranch and held it in the fire until it reddened. The other boys held Estrellita down. One sat on her legs, the other held her head, they called her Ester and pulled her hair up from her forehead. Their beer breaths spread through her nose and lungs. The boy with the branding iron leaned over her and pressed it into her forehead. Estrellita smelled her flesh burning and fainted.

She lay in the mouth of the cave for two days while the tides washed over her. The cold water trickled down her legs and prompted her to wake. "Get up, get up, and tell your parents you are all right, they are looking for you, frantic with fear." Fish swam in and out of the cave. They curled over her body with the tide, swam through her hair and over her face and were swept away. In low tide, sand covered the bottom part of her body. The tides washed her for two days, but she did not drown. When fishermen saw her lying there, they thought she was a mermaid trapped between the rocks at the mouth of the cave. One of her legs twitched as a wave ran over it and they saw that she was not a mermaid. Her black hair streamed over her face, and they did not see the mark that had been branded into her forehead. They were fearful about telling anyone about their discovery lest they be implicated, and wondered if they should let her lay there and let the ocean make the decision. She was practically drowned already. One more tide would end it. Then her gray eyes opened with a color as cold as the water she lay in. The fishermen thought she would take revenge on them from the grave now that she knew who they were, and decided it was better to take her to the hospital in Osorno. They carried her into their truck with her hands and feet bound like a sea creature and dumped her on the steps of the hospital, and fled. She was brought back to human form except for the letter on her forehead.

Her mother sat beside her bed and wept. The mark was terrible, but perhaps worse had been done to Estrellita. She was so young. They did not know how to ask her. The doctor said there was no evidence that Estrellita had been--he struggled for the right words--touched? "You don't have to worry about that." They did not believe him, nor did anyone else in the village. "As for the mark," the doctor spoke of the future as if everything could be resolved there, "when she has recovered from this trauma in a year or two, you can remove it with plastic surgery. She can still grow up to be a beautiful woman and marry and have children and a normal life."

Estrellita would never be beautiful, but she was not unattractive. She had her father's straight boney nose and his high cheekbones. Her face was angular and her lips voluptuous. Her skin and her hair were brown like her father's, but her eyes were light and belonged to another people. No one had paid attention to that before, but now everyone felt that they were chilling eyes. Something had crept into them from the ocean, the eyes of a fish had taken their place. The fishermen had felt their power on them as she lay with the tide and seaweed between her legs, but they did not speak of this, not even to each other.

Everyone believed she had been raped. Her father believed it too. It tortured him, but the letter on her forehead tortured him more. The black bang cut practically to the bridge of her nose did not hide it from him. Covering it made no difference. They brought her to a machi though Estrellita was not sick, but the medicine woman could not erase the mark.

"We do not know why they did this to her," her father said. "They branded her like an animal." But they came to know slowly, thinking about it, independently of each other, not telling each other. Rumor in the village made salient what had been ignored. Never before had their ancestors made a difference. His wife had worn the silver breastplate shaped like a hawk to the festivals, lit candles on Friday night, and said the prayers she had learned by rote from her mother.

The machi did not care about an explanation because she knew that evil spirits do not need a motive. They roam the earth in search of doing mischief for its own sake, kidnapping young girls like Estrellita to turn them into evil spirits like themselves. Her powers had prevailed against kulaka before and she was confident of success. She massaged Estrellita's forehead to make the letter go away. She rubbed it with medicine from the canelo pine and wild strawberries and pressed her thumbs into the letter until Estrellita thought the machi's thumbs would penetrate her skull. She put her lips on the letter and tried to suck it off, but it was too strong. The machi did not like to be defeated and became furious. She would have to go into a trance, which was exhausting and fraught with the danger of delirium and hallucinations. It was possible to descend and never come back. But she did not like an evil spirit to oppose her and told her assistant to prepare for her trance. She climbed a ladder to fetch light from the heavens, then descended to the ground away from the daylight, down into the mind's sweaty darkness.

Estrellita and her parents waited on the edge of a circle the machi had drawn for them to sit in. For a long hour they sat in the circle and waited to hear news of what she would bring back. A hawk flew round their circle. They sat anxiously, waiting to see whether it would fly to the left or the right, to evil or to good. After many minutes the machi ascended the ladder of returning consciousness and lifted herself out the darkness, shivering uncontrollably. Her temperature had fallen and she could not speak at first, but Estrellita and her parents had already grasped that they were fated. The hawk had flown off to their left, which was the symbol of doom. Still they were shocked when the machi looked at Estrellita with furious eyes and said, "Go away. You cannot be cured."

Estrellita fainted.

Her father stood up and made a wrathful speech about how the white man had not been able to conquer his people until they found this way. He reminded the machi how the white man could not drive the Mapuches from their lands as they had driven others. The Spaniards had come over the mountain, but when they arrived at their village they found it empty. Not a soul was there. The Mapuches had sent their women and children away and the men had gone out in canoes and hid along the coast, in and out of the inlets. Five hours they clung to branches along the coast to keep the canoes from moving. When the Spaniards came into the village, no one was there. To them the easy capitulation seemed natural. It was tempting to believe that the Indians had fled as cowards. The Spaniards made camp, unbuckled their swords and took off their armor. Nothing else stirred beside their talk and their laughter. The ocean was like a lake. They built fires and laid down to their hard sleep. Guards were posted at the roads going in and out of the village, north, south and east across the mountains. The moon was behind clouds. The night was dark and bewitching. Then the canoes slithered quietly through the water like a knife in warm butter. The waves carried the Mapuches into shore soundlessly, and they disembarked and slew the invaders. Everyone knew this story.

Now other invaders had returned and had changed his daughter into a kaluka, and everyone was afraid to be near her. The school told her not to come anymore. No one came to their door, no one sat with them at the festivals.

His partners would not fish with him, and his sons left the village. It was a terrible judgment against him. He was cut off from the living, and he believed that if he did not return to Chiloé he would be cut off from his ancestors as well. He would be stranded in time, unable to go backward or forward.

Estrellita and her mother begged him not to go. It was winter and the channels were difficult to cross, but he was more terrified of staying than of going. There was a judgment against him and his terror pushed him out into the ocean in the winter in his boat, across the cold choppy water out into the open sea, until his boat became a dot in space. Small glaciers from Patagonia that had lost their moorings floated by him. The comanchaca, the icy mist spawned by the Humboldt stream, swept across the sky and over the water. It covered the ocean and the faces of Estrellita and her mother as they stood on the shore until they could see nothing more of his boat, not even the lights of the silver steamers on the horizon where he was going. The water and the sky had swallowed him up, and swallowed up the shoreline and his village and he no longer could see it. The comanchaca was so thick he could not see to the end of his legs or see his hands in front of him. He could not see the sails on his boat or hear them flapping. There was no wind, only the dead, cold mist. Nothing moved except the fog that crept into his mouth and covered his eyes and his body with a shroud. The way through the channels disappeared, the separation between heaven and earth disappeared. One could not tell where in or out or up or down was. He lay crouched in the bottom of the boat to keep his body warm and hoped the tide would carry him to Chiloé so that he could make amends to his ancestors, but the fingers of the night stretched out, curled up, and closed him into its palm.

Estrellita's mother came down to the shore every day and every day saw his boat on the horizon coming back, as she used to see it when he returned from fishing. Every day she went down to the shore and prayed she would see the boat on the horizon coming closer and closer. But it never came closer. It remained exactly on the horizon, beyond which her eyes could not see. "What has happened to you?" she spoke to him. "Have you become a hawk? Is your soul now in the sky?"

Her sons came from Santiago and said she must leave the village, Estrellita must have an operation to remove the letter from her forehead, otherwise it was hopeless for her. "You are not fated to bear this. It is ridiculous to think that. It was the work of pranksters and nothing else. You must take your life into your hands. Then the nightmare will be over, and you won't have to see the letter anymore."

Estrellita's gray eyes stared at them beneath the black fringe and searched their faces for discernment. Did they believe she could throw off her doom by going away? When she went shopping in her own village, she now had to drop her coins into the grocer's hand as she had done in Osorno with the others. She was now a kaluka to everyone, fearful to speak with anyone but her mother. Silence wrapped her brain like the comanchaca.

Her brothers were disgusted that she could not throw off these beliefs. They prevailed upon the doctor to visit her and try to convince her to have the operation. He knew the Indian mind but agreed to try. "We will give you an anesthesia and graft some skin from your thigh or your hip," he told Estrellita and her mother. "In a year the skin will grow over your forehead and you will not see the letter anymore."

"It will always be there. The machi could not remove it. You cannot remove it."

Her response did not surprise him. An idea is like a brick wall. Nevertheless, he tried again, "My dear child, you had a terrifying experience, but you can put it behind you. Others have had terrible experiences and have put them behind them. Life beckons us. You will go elsewhere, where others will not know you."

It did not console Estrellita to go away and live among strangers. "The world cannot erase what has been done."

"The world did not do this. You cannot say the world does this or that. Only some people in the world do things, and other people do other things. You do not have to abide by what evil people do. In fact, you must not."

Her mother was exhausted with the constant pressure from her sons and the doctor. Perhaps there was a new way in the world, perhaps it was possible to remove these marks. She would try to believe it. "Go with the doctor," she told Estrellita, though her loneliness would be terrible if Estrellita went. She herself would not go. The house had roots that sprang up from the earth beneath it and would not let her move. The soul of her house was her soul. The brothers shriveled with disgust when the doctor wrote them that Estrellita had decided to stay with her mother. Life was full of answers if one threw off the past, but if they insisted on clinging to it, they would drown in it as their father had. The past was an ocean that rolled over everything. You could not fight it, you could only go somewhere else, be someone else, drown the old self like a suicide.

"Do as the doctor says," her mother pleaded after the doctor had gone. "Who will marry you with that mark? You look like an animal that is owned by someone."

Estrellita brushed the insult away. She did not want to live with either of her brothers, and where else could she go? She climbed into her mother's bed at night and clung to her. She did not know if she protected her mother or if her mother protected her. Their old friends looked the other way when they saw them, and the young boys snickered at Estrellita. But in spite of their insulting looks desire for them gripped her body. When she started to menstruate, her mother cried, "The day will soon come when you will want to marry. What can we do?"

Estrellita denied it, but her body escaped her control. She dreamed of love even though she feared the boys in the village. She picked up her bangs and flung the unerasable past at her mother. "Who will marry me?" She dared her mother to answer.

Her mother clamped her mouth shut. Here it must end. Change must come. Her past was her own burden. It must not be Estrellita's.

A day broke with a violent winter storm. In spite of this her mother put on a raincoat to go down to the ocean and stand on the shore, hoping she would see her husband's boat, demanding that her desire for him would translate into reality. Estrellita snickered like the boys, "Do you think the hawks will bring him back?"

The words scratched her mother's heart like thorns. "That is a bad thing to say, Estrellita. You have become a kaluka."

Estrellita put her hands over her ears and screamed, "Yes, yes, I have. Soon you will fear me too. Go yourself to watch for him."

"I will, I will, I will not desert him."

Sheets of rain fell everywhere and her mother could not see anything. The roads were flooded. Every trail was obliterated. The mist covered the coast and the tide rolled in with icy white waves. It was difficult to distinguish between land and water, heaven and earth. Everything was steel gray, cold and wet. The freezing water curled around her ankles, but she ignored it. Waves slapped first at her thighs, then at her breasts. The rain was so heavy that she did not know whether her body was wet from the rain or from the ocean. Estrellita's taunt drove nails into her brain. The sweet child had disappeared into the witches' world. She had a vision of the days and years to come, cut off from her sons and her daughter, from their children, from her ancestors, from the past and the future, stranded on a spit of time. She felt like a quirk of nature, like a penquin on an ice floe that had floated out of its natural climate. Nothing would ever be familiar as she drifted about without mooring in time. She walked out into the ocean and let the icy mist put its fingers down her throat.

When she did not return, Estrellita ran down to the beach to find her, then she ran to the store, hoping her mother had gone there to buy some food, but the store was shut. She ran through the village, but it was impossible to see anything. The trails were washed out, trees lay across the roads. Every boat had been pulled in from the ocean. No one was out. Premonition gripped her with steel bands. The rain beat on her like pellets. The world was washed away in water and wind. She fell on the road and lay there like one of the branches that had been felled by the wind.

In the morning someone who had weathered the storm by drinking through it found her and thought she was a seal the ocean had thrown out. She lay on her stomach with her raincoat wrapped around her legs and her head, her arms folded under her, a wet shape like a fish that had floated into the shore. When he turned her over and saw the mark on her forehead he ran through the village screaming. The villagers came, but no one would touch her. They called for an ambulance in Osorno and it took her back to the hospital. She lay drowned again for two days and could not understand why again she was saved. Her mother was gone. Her body had washed up in the morning, tangled in her father's net. There was no funeral for her because the villagers feared her as the mother of a kaluka. She would taint the earth she lay in, and they pushed her body back into the ocean. Estrellita asked that she too be thrown into the ocean. That was the fate of one who was a kaluka. There was no place on earth for them.

"You must go away," the doctor pleaded with her. "Now there is no reason to stay here. This is what your mother wanted for you. Don't refuse her gift. You are entitled to marry and have children. You are entitled to a life. This is the only medicine I can give you. I am going to call your brothers and tell them to come and get you. Don't live here anymore."

She became feverish and delirious. "Throw me into the ocean," she wept. "I know where her soul came from and I know where it went, throw me in too and let my soul go back to hers."

The trip to Santiago was twenty-six hours. Estrellita sat next to her brother and scarcely moved the whole time. The doctor gave her a pill to ease her pain. Sometimes she looked as if she had fallen asleep, otherwise she sat upright and rigid. She and her brother looked like an odd couple, she with her Indian clothes and he obviously a man of the city. She was attractive, even though her forehead was covered with ugly bangs. Underneath her bowler hat, her face was both severe and seductive. People gazed at her with the sympathy or disdain reserved for cholitos who find their way into the city, wondering why she would leave her birthplace and come to Santiago. Everyone knew what happened to most young girls like her who left their villages to come to the city. The streets were filled with them. Her brother felt conspicuous, aware of the contrast between them and of the speculations strangers might make about their relationship. Santiago was filled with pimps who brought girls like Estrellita to the city. He hadn't considered how they would look together until he found himself sitting next to her on the train under the gaze of strangers. Beneath her cape she wore her mother's silver breast piece. The memory of their angry last words to each other crept like fiery ants over her brain.

When her brother brought her into his apartment, she did not hear what he or his wife said to her. For weeks she heard only her inner remorseful voices. She heard nothing but what was in her head and sat grim and silent for weeks in the bedroom they had prepared for her. She listened to the ocean roar and the rain hiss, and practiced a militant stoicism against efforts to take her to see the city or be introduced to people or go shopping for new clothes. Her presence began to haunt their lives and her brother's wife could not bear it anymore. "She does nothing but sit in a chair and stare. She should go to school, let me take her to the stores and buy her something to wear so she can walk in the streets and not look like an Indian." She did not apologize for the remark. "She should get a job, something to get her out of her room, make her go out into the world."

"What sort of job can she get without an education? You know what happens to girls like her."

His wife took the initiative. She worked in a nursing home and there were plenty of requests for girls like Estrellita. In a few days she found a job for her in someone's home, a woman whose husband was her patient.

"It's a few blocks from here, a short walk through the park, a woman by the name of Mrs. Schwartz. You can start tomorrow. I will go with you and show you the way. You cannot sit like this anymore, Estrellita. Do you understand? This is not what your mother died for."

Her words broke the circle Estrellita had drawn about the memory of her mother's death. What if she told them that her words had driven her mother out of the house because she was a kaluka. They would regard her as mad, yet there was no other explanation. No one could explain it anymore than they could explain the mark on her forehead. How could she go about in a city where no one understood her?

"I am sorry," her sister-in-law said, "but you cannot sit like this in this room anymore."

The next morning she took Estrellita to show her the way across the park to Mrs. Schwartz' apartment, where Estrellita would help Mrs. Schwartz whose husband was sick with a disease that affected his memory. He was in the nursing home, and his wife brought him home every Friday for the weekend. She needed someone to help her with him when he was home. Estrellita came from Thursday to Sunday to clean the house and help put him in his wheelchair, wheel him through the park, prop him up at the table and feed him.

When she came in the morning, the apartment looked as if Mrs. Schwartz had not been there at all. Nothing seemed touched. The couch and the chairs seemed never to have been sat in. Occasionally she found a cup in the sink with some leftover coffee. She dusted the clean furniture, changed the linen on Friday, and polished the candlesticks which were on the piano with the photographs of Mrs. Schwartz' family, her daughter, her son-in-law and grandchildren who lived in Australia, her wedding picture and a picture of her husband in a white suit bowing in front of a piano. "He was a concert pianist," Mrs. Schwartz explained. "The picture was taken in Berlin, in 1937." She mourned her husband's shattered talent. His hands now played on the empty air, searching for a keyboard. His eyes fluttered constantly, swung back and forth as they looked for something recognizable to take hold of. Estrellita understood his problem.

"Is she my daughter?" he once asked his wife. Mrs. Schwartz did not answer. She told Estrellita it did not matter whether they answered him or not. "He doesn't remember anything. It's a sickness." She laughed ruefully, "Or maybe a mercy. Who can say?"

Sometimes Estrellita sat in the park where there were other Indian girls like herself, carrying laundry and bundles off to housework somewhere. She did not know where they came from or if they would recognize her as a kaluka. Every morning she wetted her bangs and pasted them down on her forehead.

One day an Indian man sat down on the bench next to her. He was there the next morning and sat down next to her again, his head inclined at an angle of interest. She was fearful that he would recognize her as a kaluka. He was there whenever she was there, even when she went home in the evening. He did not seem to fear her as the men in her village feared her, but he showed the same dark interest. His presence on the same bench each morning became a landmark for her, the place where her eyes looked instantly along the path she took. If he was not there she wondered if she had missed her path. He was the same age as her brother, and like him did not wear Indian clothes. Where had he come from? Where did he go when he wasn't there? She did not ask him questions when he sat down on the bench next to her. He asked the questions. "How long have you been in Santiago?" And smiled. "Let me see, you have probably been here about three months. You come from the South. Your mother and father have died. You are alone or living with a brother who left the village or the reservation." And smiled at her amazed eyes. She was not bad looking, except for her bangs. He reached out to brush them up and she backed away. He noted the vulnerability to touch, and reported to Madame that she was a virgin.

"That will only fetch a good price once," she said. "It would be better to break her in."

The next day he picked up one of her fingers and caressed it. Her body trembled. Oh, what a virgin! Imagine if he caressed her entire body. Estrellita could not imagine it. He caressed her fingers one by one and in the valleys between each finger, not in the same way as Mr. Schwartz did when he held her hand in his like a blind man groping for something familiar, or stared at her face as if each day it was unfamiliar. One day he reached for her face with a surprisingly swift movement and brushed up her bangs. The red letter was moist from her hair and looked like the bite of a vampire, the iconic mark of a legend no one is supposed to believe in. "What's that?" he rasped. "Is that an Indian marking? Is that what you people do to yourselves? No, don't tell me. I don't want to know."

It terrified him at first sight, but he went through a surprising revolution. The letter beneath her bangs transformed itself into something else. It disappeared as a letter and re-emerged as a clef on a sheet of music. All day it floated before his eyes, sometimes upside down with the curve on the top, sometimes right side up. He came to believe that her body was covered with musical notes. When he looked at her his fingers remembered Chopin and they flooded with music under his fingernails to their very tips. He wanted to see her naked so that he could read the musical scores on her belly and her breasts. Melodies crept back into his hands. "You never lose muscle memory," he told her, his fingers itching to take off her clothes, "or bone memory. The body knows. The body always knows whatever it has ever known. You can't escape that. Maybe the brain forgets," he laughed, "but the body never forgets. My fingers have never forgotten anything they have ever played."

As soon as Estrellita came into the apartment, his hands played Chopin in the air. He read her face as he used to read his music sheets and began to play. He couldn't walk and had to be fed, but he could play music again. He told his wife that with more time to practice she would be able to wheel him into a concert hall, place Estrellita next to him and he would be able to play. "I don't even need a piano. Because it's all there, under her bangs, all the music I used to play. It's all there, Beethoven, Mozart, Schumann. She has hundreds of music scores tattooed under her bangs."

A chill went through Mrs. Schwartz. Step by step she had gone down the slope of madness with her husband, bolstered at each step by medical explanations that soon evaporated. Now his doctor had nothing to say about this new turn of the screw in her husband's demented state, except that the illusion did not seem to be doing him any harm. His lack of curiosity exasperated her. She believed that he had run out of his prop of rationalizations and was tired of her husband's case. What difference did one more illusion make?

"Let me see your forehead," Mrs. Schwartz demanded of Estrellita on several occasions.

No, no, no. Estrellita was adamant, but so was Mrs. Schwartz. Estrellita's stubbornness whetted her determination to see what was under her bangs. Finally she said she would dismiss her if she did not show her what was there. To spite her, Estrellita lifted her bangs, believing the sight would punish Mrs. Schwartz for pursuing her unmercifully. She was not wrong. A red wave rushed into Mrs. Schwartz' mouth and drowned her with blood. History collapsed into a single letter. Estrellita would not explain how she came to have it on her forehead. She would not tell Mrs. Schwartz she was a kaluka. Mrs. Schwartz would not understand. No, Mrs. Schwartz would not understand. Like everyone else she thought the mark could be removed. She learned the story in the nursing home from Estrellita's sister-in-law, how Estrellita had been kidnapped and that she refused to remove the mark. "Indian superstitions," the sister-in-law said apologetically.

"That does not explain it," Mrs. Schwartz said heatedly.

"I cannot drag her to a hospital," the sister-in-law retorted angrily because she detected blame.

"It must be removed," Mrs. Schwartz said with surprising intensity. "It must be removed," she repeated to Estrellita. Fury foamed on her lips. "Do you understand? You don't have to live with what evil people do to you."

She sat at her husband's bedside and wryly watched his fingers diddle on the air because he believed there were musical notes on Estrellita's forehead. What did one more illusion matter? She was revolted. Not this illusion. Estrellita must have the letter removed even if it destroyed her husband's consolation.

"It cannot be removed," Estrellita said, spitting out her fate.

Mrs. Schwartz' chest tightened. Bile flooded into her mouth. "It is the sign of evil people. Evil people! Do you understand? You must not give in to evil people. You must not allow them to determine the world for you." Having sworn that she would never look at them again, she took out an album of pictures, "See this girl, younger than you. That is me. See my arm, see the numbers on it.

That's what evil people did to me, but I had it removed, I had it removed, and you must too. I will give you the money for the operation, and go with you to see that it is properly done. You must not allow evil people to put their mark on you."

Estrellita refused with as much force as Mrs. Schwartz insisted. Everyday Mrs. Schwartz argued with her to have the operation, while her husband pleaded with her to cut her bangs off or take her clothes off. "Show me, show me," he said, stretching out his hands to an invisible piano. "Show me the music on your body." Mrs. Schwartz screamed at him that he was revolting. This did not deter him. " I know I will be able to play again if she will let me see her body." His wife did not understand and he hated her for cutting him off from his powers.

"You are making my husband more sick," she said to Estrellita. "You see how he behaves when you enter his bedroom." Yes, Estrellita saw, she understood: it was the power of the kaluka, but she did not tell that to Mrs. Schwartz, and did not come back.

The next morning she sat on the bench in the park and let her Indian friend play with her fingers. Mr. Schwartz howled. His fingers hung suspended in the air, searching for the keyboard and stiffening with their ache to remember and play while Estrellita walked along the river with her new friend. She did not tell him why she did not go to work that morning, and he didn't care. They walked along the river, and through parks. He sensed that she was troubled, but he was patient. He put his arm around her waist. She stiffened and unbent at the same time, trembled and restrained herself. Oh, what a virgin! They would cut her hair and dress her to look like a city woman. Maybe not. Madame would know best. It wasn't up to him to say what to do with her. There was only one thing that was up to him.

"You look tired," he said. "I have a place where we can rest. You will feel better if you rest a while." He found a hotel along the river where he was known, no questions asked, his work familiar. Same room, same girl, different name. He told her to lay down on the bed and after a while lay down next to her and parted her trembling thighs. "She's not half bad looking," he thought, except for her hair," and kept her for himself for a few weeks.

"Where's that girl?" Madame asked, suspicious that he was stealing fruits.

"She's difficult," he said, which was partly true. Estrellita still trembled. She trembled with anticipation and fear because she lost control of her body. When he came near, her body leaped at him and shocked her. He laughed with double pleasure because he was also putting it over on Madame, but it had to end and she had to be pruned. One day while she was sleeping, he rested on an elbow and picked up her bangs to see how she would look if they were cut. Her eyes opened immediately. He leaped from the bed, not sure what he was looking at, not sure if Madame would accept her with a scar like that. "Goddamit!"

Estrellita burst into tears.

"Stop it," he screamed at her, judging that he had lost the fruits of his labor. "Put your bangs down again." He had to tell Madame, who took it with more equanimity. "Let me have a look at the girl. You never can tell. Men have strange desires. If she is as good as you say, it might be in her favor." When she saw Estrellita with her gray eyes as sharp as jewels, her sensuous lips, she parted her bangs and judged that the letter might be an attraction in such a face. Contradictions were always interesting. Maybe in the street the letter would be a mark against her, but in her house which catered to the otré, Estrellita might find the hard-to-please client who required his imagination to be jolted by primitive vistas.

Her house was in the center of Valparaiso, on a hill where it overlooked the last harbor in the world. Nineteenth century houses from colonial days stretched along the quay. The house was surrounded by gardens and a wrought iron fence and guarded by dogs and private police. It was furnished sumptuously and wittily, according to Madame's sense of humor. Each room represented another country or city, China, Russia, Germany, England, the United States, Mexico, Paraguay, Chile, Argentina, Saudi Arabia, Egypt. Madame explained that they hosted diplomats and tourists, many of whom were not comfortable in a foreign setting or many who were not comfortable in a familiar setting. "For the Englishman who needs an Italian or Arabian room, we have just the thing," she said, taking Estrellita around. "For the Egyptian who needs an English room or the Nile, we have just the thing with an appropriate girl. We can accommodate the German who needs a Russian room or the Russian who needs a Chinese room. We have twenty different rooms, twenty different nations, twenty different destinies. It's all a matter of what tickles their fancy. But where shall we put you? We do not have an Indian room." She looked at Estrellita's gray eyes and surmised foreign strains in her blood. Madame was thrifty and shrewd. Her investments were carefully planned. Nothing happened without an exact accounting. Should she lay out the expense to create an Indian room for a crossbreed? But Madame was also witty. Her rooms were full of sobering comic effects. The Englishman whose room was filled with rococo murals of Nelson and coronation ceremonies felt gratified and amused, he liked to take his national ardor as a joke; and the Frenchman did not mind the scenes from the Revolution with its guillotine and timbrels because he appreciated that glory had its price in blood and scandal. For the Germans there were two rooms, one painted with opera scenes from Wagner's work and one with scenes from Goethe reading Faust.

She was inventive and controlled everything. She had meals catered and groceries delivered, she had her own medical staff and gardeners. The house was self-contained, spacious, built of white stucco, with a surrounding porch in the style of a governor's mansion, and a garden filled with gardenias. Everyone knew what the house was, and that amused them too because the men who came were flattered that their needs, personal and historical, were thought of. A Russian would be fed Russian food in his Russian room or, if he preferred he could have a western-style sandwich. Madame employed four cooks who labored in two kitchens, a separate kitchen for Jews and Muslims who would not be able to eat in her establishment if pork touched their chicken or milk touched their beef.

Estrellita disappeared into Valparáiso, and neither her brothers nor Mrs. Schwartz could find her. Her name never appeared in a police or hospital record. If they suspected that she had been kidnapped the police were puzzled to know how they could find her. Santiago was filled with girls who looked like her. The distinctive scar on her forehead did not matter. How could they recognize her by this if she always covered it? Could they go about lifting up the hair of all the women in Santiago?

Madame did not ask Estrellita to cut her bangs, only to lift them to any client who asked her to do that. She built an Indian room with a mural of the famous poem of the Auracanians, depicting battle scenes between the Mapuche and the Spanish. Chileans liked this room because they respected the Mapuche whom they had conquered. One man became infatuated with Estrellita as "the real thing," except, of course, for her gray eyes. Madame's intuition and investment paid off. Word got around and soon other men besides the Chileans asked for Estrellita. Her gray eyes in her dark skin chilled and heated their imagination at the same time. The woman had a secret on her forehead and in her eyes and between her thighs which caused Madame's clients to roar with pleasure. Estrellita's thighs no longer trembled, she now exercised control over her body. She could grasp a client's torso between her legs like a prey in the talons of a hawk, while all the time her eyes stared into his face as she memorized it, the dark skinned, the light skinned, the pockmarked, the smooth skinned. Each face fell down into her soul. Her eyes were gray flint that sent flaming shudders into them. They did not even mind her absurd haircut. It betokened her primitive caste to them which here they appreciated. Sometimes a client would brush her bangs up and was startled by what he found. Some were shocked. Was that the sign of an Indian ritual? She never explained. Some were revolted and did not ask for her again. Madame did not mind, because most of the men did. One man was so inflamed by the mark each time he saw Estrellita he picked up her bangs and licked the letter with his tongue until it aroused him to orgasm. A Russian tried to bite it off. An Englishman told Madame that Estrellita would look more civilized if she had it removed.

"Does that mean you won't request her anymore?" Madame asked, who didn't mind because Estrellita was constantly booked by everyone, Chinese, Japanese, Frenchmen, Swedes. They were titillated by the letter, enflamed by it, intrigued by it, revolted by it, but always aroused. The Englishman hesitated fastidiously, then said with a measured voice to impress Madame that he was weighing the situation, "I didn't say that."

One man had a catastrophic experience. On the edge of his orgasm, the anticipation surging in his blood, Estrellita's bangs accidentally parted and the "J" leaped out at him moist and red. His organ deflated immediately. He clutched at her breasts, wondering what happened. Still he returned again, but with a warning: "Make sure I don't see it" he said, parting her legs.

One man thought it was a divine sign, another a taboo. One man said he knew it was a judgment on him, but he could not help himself. The sight of the letter turned his blood to a fire which enthralled him, emotions he had never felt, did not want to feel, soared in him, and he blamed Estrellita for it. He demanded that Madame throw her out so he could have some peace. His fury pleased her. You could not distress Madame as long as she made money.

For many, it did not matter how they saw the letter, as long as they saw it. They would sweep Estrellita's hair up, stare with astonishment as if they did not know it was going to be there, and groan. It always activated an ecstasy in them that shuddered down into their groins, while she thrust her mind elsewhere, back to her house in the village, back to the forest, back to the ocean where the salt had run through her blood and the spray had wet her lips as her father turned his boat towards shore before the night curled up its fist.

Finally a German came who had heard rumors of a woman in this house with a "J' on her forehead. Was this a joke? In such an establishment? Did Madame understand what the mark was? Madame said she understood that it was good for business and if he didn't like it he did not have to have Estrellita. He said he would pay to look at her without touching her. Madame shrugged her shoulders and took his money. Estrellita lay on the bed while he sat in a chair and stared at her with a confusing expression and a confusing request. He told her to part her bangs, not her thighs. "That's what I paid for," he said. Then he bent over her and pressed his thumb into her forehead like a branding iron. The memory of the night she had been kidnapped flashed through her brain like a lightning streak and wiped out the room she was laying in, the murals, the furnishings, the objects of sexual seduction. Her eyes swung in her head and tried to look at anything but his white moon face, but she couldn't. He took her chin in his hand and kept her face immobilized. She could not look anywhere else. He would not let her. He pressed his lips on her forehead and stroked the letter with his tongue until the heat rose in his organ. But it would not release him. He lay panting on her breast, his hand clutching her chin, his tongue licking the letter, but he could not find release. His sexual energy ran back into his body like a poisoned river. She tried to throw him off, but she couldn't. She lay imprisoned under his weight until her body became as wooden as a puppet's.

Afterwards she became useless. The men began to complain about her. Not even the letter on her forehead could revive their interest in her. She was dead. When she went outdoors, she could not smell the gardenias, she could not hear the traffic, she could not see the sun. She did not know where to put her eyes to find a world she wanted to look at. Her body was forgetting life. She knew that this was the end because the body never forgets anything while it is alive.

One night she walked down a flight of broken steps and broken streets filled with cats. She made her way into the ocean and let the water rise above her thighs, then above her hips, then her breasts. The waves played between her fingers like the pimp used to play with them. That was what her body remembered, and she closed her hand into a fist. All her memories were bad. "You are a kaluka," her mother had said. If she walked out far enough, maybe she would find her mother who would say something else to her now. She drifted until her feet could not reach the bottom and her head bobbed on the waves like a ball under the moonlight. She was not sure how to drown, but she felt if she walked out far enough it must happen. And it did. A wave rushed into her mouth. To her surprise she began to thrash frantically. It was hard to drown. The body could not forget its life, after all. Even though it no longer felt anything, it fought against the wishes of her soul. But in the end her soul was stronger and she held her body down until the water crawled through her lungs and pushed the air out of her body and put out its fires, its desire to live, to know love, to have children. Her hair floated up from her face and revealed to the incurious fish its granite shape with the letter on her forehead. The souls of her mother and father

floated on the bottom of the ocean. She made her way towards them with outstretched hands. But everyone knows the dead are cold shapes, they cannot console, and Estrellita sank until her body disappeared.

#

EPITAPH FOR AN AGE

I am not one of those who were taken away in the boxcars. I am one of those who watched the boxcars go by. I am not one of those who were callous. I am one of those who believed that there are more good people in the world than bad, but that the bad have strength because they know what they hate. Evil people collect together. They smell each other out and run together like pus in a sore. Good people are dispersed; they are private. They have nothing for which to collect together. Therefore, it seemed to me that if good is to overcome evil, for once, in our time, good people must bring themselves together with the force of an implosion that will weld them together identifiably and that, if only as witnesses to their indestructible will to make over the earth in their image, will scatter the haters like sand.

What are our weapons? Only our willpower.

My grandfather and my father were political revolutionaries of a mild sort. More important, they were men of conscience, trained to the motto that all that it took for evil to triumph was for good men to do nothing. "Good men," my father used to say, "must be like camp followers. They must follow the army into battle and pitch their tents on the battlefield. Good men," he used to say, "must be like the dog Argus with a hundred eyes, never sleeping. Good men must be like Janus, looking into heaven and hell at the same time. It is not enough to have principles, to catch a glimpse of Utopia. Even as you are peeking, someone is lowering the curtain. Good men must renounce their very lives, even as did the disciples of Jesus, for the battle against evil will not be won with lesser measures."

In 1891, when our district government brought in the army to put down a strike by our miners, my grandfather was one of those who sat in the entrance to the mine for six days without food. He was the first, but soon another man joined him and another. My father who was a small boy at the time, told me how he could remember his father, who was a doctor, a professional man always in impeccable clothes, his beard trimmed to a point, his monocle set in his eye like the moon in the sky, was covered with dust and soot. Someone spat on him. He did not move a muscle. His monocle was broken. There was a cut on his eyebrow. One of the army men poked him in the ribs with his bayonet. Half the town cheered. The other half crept by at night and whispered gratitude. "Stand up and be counted," my grandfather said. The next day the lawyer joined him. "Well, Sturmann," he said to my grandfather, "you did not show up for your chess game, so I had no choice." He crossed his long legs under him and sat down. Within a few minutes, I assure you, his white shirt was not white. My father told me how he watched from behind a bush and wept. At night he crawled to my grandfather and wept again. "Fear nothing," my grandfather said, "it is only people."

When my grandfather died and my father buried him, I was already a grown boy. My father looked like a man who had been given the heaviest inheritance a man could have. I doubt whether the father of the Hebrew race felt so heavy a responsibility for the future.

I did not fight in the First World War. I was eligible for the army, but my father "spirited" me out of Germany. He put me on a small boat going towards France and I made my way into Switzerland, where I stayed for the duration of the war. "We shall yet rescue the world," my father said to me the night I left. He gripped my shoulders. The night was as dark as tar and we could only feel and hear each other. I felt, in that darkness, my father's passion for pacifism, and I have never borne arms. Indeed, I gave up eating meat more than ten years ago, despising death and all acts connected with death.

You see from what stock I come. We are determined that good will be consummate and that evil, because it is a disease and self-destroying, cannot be. We are determined not to be lax, not to be seduced by fatalism or primitive remains of Manicheanism. This compulsion has driven our family since the time of Our Lord Jesus Himself. And we are determined to take our final rest in His belief that good is omnipotent and evil is powerless before its finest statement.

When the boxcars first appeared in our town late on an August evening in 1942, we were confused as to what they meant. They were sealed. They stopped only for minutes. They came from the west and went east. But when they came by again in October, we were alert with rumors. Some of our townspeople had been to the eastern border, had been at the depot when the train pulled in. "People," they said, "people are on the trains."

My wife, I must admit, laughed at first. "Circus people," she said. "A new act."

Schunken, a man of indifferent disposition who didn't care one way or the other, shrugged his shoulders. As far as he was concerned he was merely reporting what he saw. He didn't care what my wife thought, but his companion wiped his nose on his sleeve, twirled his cap, and clearly felt the hand of God in his ribs. "A new act," he said, "yes, but these weren't circus people as far as I could see. When they opened the doors half of them fell out dead."

My friend, Kernfeffer, was at my house that evening. He moved to the edge of his chair. "You don't mean really dead?" he said.

"You can call it what you want," Schunken said, "but they never moved again. They were shoveled onto a truck and taken away."

There is a hill on my farm from which I can see perhaps a mile of track, so when the train came through in October I saw it coming before anyone else did. I was harvesting and working hard. Nevertheless, I felt something hit my forehead as if someone had thrown a pebble into my brain. I looked up and saw the train on the horizon. How many trains pass through Oberpassen? Perhaps six a day, four passenger and two freight. There was no reason for this train to capture my attention. But it did. I watched it wriggle on the horizon like a dancing worm, something for a child's cartoon, something unreal that had been animated. It was so undistinguished. I watched it come closer as one should watch a tornado come in from an open field, uncertain what it is until its reality is impassable. Not till the train passed did it dawn on me. Every car was sealed. There was no writing anywhere, no information, no freight description, no weight, no destination markings. Not a sign of freight or passenger, its message sealed like a tomb. I jumped into my truck and drove to the station as fast as I could. It was not fast enough. "Stop it," I shouted as it pulled away. "There are live men and women sealed into that train. Stop it, stop it." I got into my truck and drove to the home of our priest. He was at dinner, reading his mail.

There were tears in his eyes. "Have you heard," he asked, "our monastery in Northern India was washed away by the floods. Three hundred people perished in the town. We have lost Father Holgen and Sister Margaret." He crossed himself, but his lips were trembling with sorrow.

"That is a disaster," I said, "but I was not referring to that." I told him how I had seen another train of boxcars go by such as had gone by in August, and how Schunken had said he had been at the depot when it had arrived because he had a delivery over the border and saw how the cars had contained live men and women.

"Schunken, Schunken!" our priest said. "What does Schunken know? Who can believe such an idiot. When Schunken was a little boy he once said he had seen a cat burned alive come back again."

"But the whole countryside is filled with these rumors," I said. "By now, others have seen. Not only Schunken."

"What others?" he shouted. He was clearly upset over the news from India. Father Holgen had been a friend of his and he had known Sister Margaret from infancy, had directed her feet to India. "Have you seen? Has your wife seen? Have I seen? Who has seen? Rumors! I remember when I was a little boy someone said the world was coming to an end. Everyone ran to the top of the mountain. Two people died of heart failure. The next day, everyone came down from the mountain." He covered his eyes with his hands so that I would not see him weeping. "Go away, Sturmann," he said, "unless you have some evidence besides Schunken's word. Imagine if I brought the matter to the council and said, Schunken says. We are surrounded by mountains with only the train route out. Better pray that the mines keep working and the mountains or the dam don't fall on your head."

I left.

My wife noticed my preoccupation and I told her what was bothering me. "If it is true—," I said.

"If it is true," she said.

"But we must act on one supposition or the other. If they are carrying legitimate freight why shouldn't the cars be labeled?"

She smiled in that way that meant she was patronizing a stupidity of mine. "If there were really something sinister, something so evil, evil people could surely practice the simple deception of falsifying freight labels. Nothing could draw more attention than the fact that the cars are not labeled, so it must be innocent. Only innocent people would act so stupidly."

There was something reasonable in that, but on the other hand it was unreasonable for anyone not to label the cars. And the innocent and the not innocent would profit from labeling. In my mind's eye I saw the train drawing across the countryside, nondescript and very usual-looking, yet ghostly. Surely I thought, if it were anything really evil,

I would know it. If we are not capable of distinguishing good from evil, how can we claim to know God whom we identify as good, how can our priests, our clergy claim to fight evil if they do not know what it is, how can the Pope be God's vicar if he cannot fight evil.

I had heard terrible stories from my father and my grandfather of massacres of Jews during the Middle Ages, burning of so-called witches, and in our own time, slavery and lynching of black men. I always believed I would know the evil thing when I saw it, because you could hear the cry of the tortured, you could smell the death in a starving child, you could feel the weight of slave chains, you could see the body swinging in the tree. The sun should not be more visible to the eye of man than that which is evil. I made up my mind that the solution was to halt the trains the next time they came through and to investigate.

The next day I had two appointments. The first was to take my wife to the doctor. She was not feeling well, was bloated and had lost her appetite. The second was to bring a request to our court for an injunction to stop the train the next time it came through town. I had to sit through three hours of deliberation about the mine union, about the nightmarish condition in our mental institution (a twelve-year-old girl had been raped by one of the guards), about the ever growing ominous problem of unemployment in our southern district. Klinger, who presided over the council, asked me on what grounds I wished to halt the trains. I repeated the story, the rumors, Schunken's eyewitness account, his companion's evidence. I exploded. "It's for the purpose of getting evidence," I shouted, "that I wish to stop the trains."

He said the matter would be considered, and they would let me know in seven days. When I left, a few of my friends pressed me to come to a meeting that evening concerning the unemployment problem. "You know very well," they said, industry is moving north for the cheap labor. We must have a statewide wage system, we must have a permanent industry residence law. It should not be easier for a man to pick up his business and ruin the working lives of thousands than for a man to divorce his wife. A man should be able to count on his livelihood like he counts on his family." I could not agree more. I had seen what unemployment could do to people. In some cases, men left their families to search for work and were never heard of again.

I passed the mine on my way to the meeting that night. In the dark the opening to the shaft looked like the hole into hell. I could imagine if I tripped and fell, I would fall forever, though I knew very well that twenty feet down was a landing. I remember my father's story of my grandfather sitting in the entrance. Only his body said no to the darkness. I had to do something about the trains, whether the court approved or not. We were twenty-seven thousand people in town, I thought. If we all stood by the station and let out a mighty roar, who would put down our voices. Stop, we would shout. Twenty-seven thousand voices. God, would you hear us? I felt my father's hand on my shoulder as on the night I left Germany. "We will yet rescue the world," he whispered in the dark.

Our meeting was disrupted by two youths who were sending around a petition to stop the war in East Africa. The chairman called for order. "We can only solve one problem at a time," he said. "We are trying to solve the problem of unemployment in our own backyard."

One of the young men jumped on a chair and shouted, "Provincial pacifists. All you care about is how to feed yourselves while your bullets are killing babies, your army is destroying villages, your bombs have torn up a country. Over twenty thousand children wander homeless. More children have been orphaned by you in this war than you have people in this town. Three times the number of civilians have been killed than you have people in this town, over ten times your numbers have been killed as soldiers on both sides, and all you're concerned with is a job. Unemployment is not famine, unemployment is not cholera, unemployment is not bullets. We can manage unemployment."

"He's right," I shouted from my feet. "What is the use of our petty concerns for our own welfare. All over the world people are dying of starvation. Here we quibble over how much social security a man needs to keep his house."

The chairman banged for order. "Charity begins at home," someone muttered. "I cannot see how it helps one starving man or woman on the other side of the world," the chairman said, "whatever it is we do here."

Of course, he was right, and once the mood of bitterness passed in me, I said so out loud. "I merely wanted to let him be heard," I said. "Of course, we should solve our own problems, but we must keep our perspective."

When I left the meeting one of the youths approached me outside the hall and asked if I would come to a protest rally they were holding a week from that night. I signed the petition and said that I would be glad to go. I asked them if they knew anything about the boxcars.

"What boxcars?" they said. They had heard nothing. I explained the situation, the incidents to them. They were very interested and asked me to get more information for them. At last I had struck fire in someone, and I went to their rally with curiosity as to who else would be there.

It was held on a farm outside the town limits, not even near a main highway. Clearly it was not a popular cause, which whet my appetite all the more. Still when I got there, I was surprised at the large numbers of people who had found their way out there. There was a platform to a side with flags and loudspeakers. A man of about thirty was making an impassioned speech against the war. In the center of the rally, a group of about forty boys and girls were doing a slow snake dance, weaving in and out silently. It was clearly symbolic of the dance of death, and their expressions, their silence, the lack of music or rhythm of any kind, the sheer repetition of the silent weaving had effect. People stepped aside to let them through. Knots of people dissolved before their advance. There were many who had come out of curiosity, as at any rally. There were even those who had come for the purpose of disrupting or propagandizing their cause, but no one disrupted or ridiculed these silent weavers in their dance of death. After they passed by, ranks closed again. I recognized Sister Mary Theresa carrying a collection box to raise money for the flood victims of Rasinpur and to rebuild the monastery. She carried a sign on her back which was meant to read: Help Your Brother Christians. But someone had crossed out the word Christians. I could imagine who did this because those involved with this protest rally were known to have hostile feelings about religion. Some of these called themselves the New Fraternity of Free Men, and I could readily think that Father Muhler had sent Sister Mary Theresa to this very rally for the purpose of reminding Christians of their Christian duty. She looked beset like a dour countess at a carnival, not sure whether to draw attention to herself or not. There was a Leninist faction seated at the back, cross legged on the ground, their hair shaved in the shape of the star of China. They carried only one placard: Life is Revolution.

I spotted my friend, Kernfeffer. "What are you doing here?"

"Same as you. How is your wife?"

"Not well. We thought she was pregnant, but it seems not to be. The doctors are now in disagreement."

"So, make her pregnant and put the doctors in agreement. Any word on the boxcars?"

"I'll know tomorrow. The court will give me a decision." I pulled him aside. "You know very well," I whispered, "what the decision will probably be. Everyone in the country has been talking, but the courts are deaf."

"Still it's nothing but rumors."

"But the rumors must be investigated. If there is any truth to them, my God, do you realize the malignancy."

"If, if, if. Last year they evacuated the town. They said the dam was going to break. We stayed away for three days." He shrugged his shoulders. "But when there was an explosion in the mine and twenty miners were killed, there were no rumors to precede it. I tell you what I think. When true evil comes it does not advertise itself. People talk up the thing that is not so bad."

"But you would agree that we must investigate."

He dropped ash from his cigar. "All right, so I agree."

"If the court does not give me a permit, what shall we do?"

He looked up at the sun. "Let us cross that bridge when we come to it."

We left the rally together. I signed a petition to permit our medical staff to give aid to the enemy. When I arrived home, I did not like at all how my wife looked. Her eyes were sunken. "Come, come, come," I said, "you are thinking the worst possible things. I know what you are thinking." My ears went cold as I spoke. "A doctor once told me more people die of the fear of the disease than of the disease itself. You mustn't let your mind run away like this."

I had intended to go to a meeting of the miners' union, but I crossed the idea out. It was absolutely essential to divert my wife. I insisted we go out for dinner and to a picture show. I met Hausner the next day who scolded me for not going to the meeting. "You think because you are not a miner and your family have not been miners this is no affair of yours. Here the mine is the economy of the district. What happens to the mines is everyone's business."

Of course, he was right and I told him so. I explained that my wife was sick. "You should take her to a clinic," he said. "These doctors here know nothing." I had suggested this to her, but she had burst into tears and had said, "I will die here where I was born. I will not go to a clinic where they experiment on you. If I am to suffer, I will suffer and die, but I will stay where I am."

My scalp prickled when she spoke this way. I became breathless and could not talk to her. I could not stand to feel that there was something seriously wrong with her. I told her she was being unreasonable. There were other diseases in the world, most of them not drastic. She could be suffering anything from an ulcer to an obscure virus, which only a clinic had the means of diagnosing properly. But she would not be budged. Fear had given her a pernicious obstinacy, a longing only for the familiar that could not be satiated. She would stand by the window and stare at a tree for hours. She walked and walked through the streets and alleys she had known as a child. Once she had found a mouse, put him in a cage, and sat all afternoon watching him. "How is it he has never seen me before and he fears me? Is fear more natural than love?"

I told Hausner I would do my best to make the next meeting and went to the court to hear about the decision to stop the trains. I had to sit for several hours hearing evidence about the guard, Blinghoffer, who had raped a demented child. They were both there. She giggled and hiccoughed, he twisted his hat in his hands and said he had meant no harm. The child's mother screamed that he was the demented one, not her daughter. It cost her half her husband's salary to keep her daughter in a private institution. The guard's mother said maybe the girl was not as demented as all that if she could get her son. The child's mother flung her fury and said a stone could get her son. The judge rapped for order. Damages were awarded to the child's mother and the guard was removed from his job. My own petition was heard out in four minutes. The said train should be halted and searched in the town of Oberpassen. Schunken alone was called to give evidence. His companion had moved to another district. Schunken repeated what he had said in the past and the case was dismissed.

Kernfeffer called me that evening. "Well?" he said.

"Dismissed," I said. "Meet me tomorrow for lunch."

"You have a private plan?" Kernfeffer asked.

I leaned across the lunch table towards him when we met. "You have a friend who works in the station house in Berlin."

"True."

"Kernfeffer, get him to give us a timetable on every train movement through here. Somewhere the boxcars must be on record. They must be on someone's report."

"What will you do when you get it?"

"If I know in advance when one is due, we will get every responsible organization in town, the Youth Movement, the Pacifist Organization, the Movement of Moral Men, the Brotherhood of Unity, collectively, to come down to the station, if need be spread our bodies across the tracks and demand that the doors be opened. We will stop those trains."

Kernfeffer is a laconic man who likes to affect a lack of sentimentality, but I knew he was with me. I had only to wait until he made connection and brought me information. In the meantime, I had much work to do. I spoke, argued, and wrote to every organization in our district that I knew I could count on. Within a week we had flyers out: Unseal The Boxcars. Tombs On Wheels. The Dying Pass Silently Through Our Town. My wife stood at the window one night and nodded her head. "There it is now." I looked out and there in the January snow was a black ribbon moving over the countryside. It could have been a train from a child's story. If it had tooted a bell it would have changed the countryside into a pastoral. But it came silently.

"How did you know?" I asked. "You cannot see whether there is writing on the cars or not in the dark."

She sighed and put on a shawl. "I had a premonition."

"Maybe you're wrong."

"I don't think so."

"Where are you going?"

"Down to the station. I wish to see if my instincts are right." She swallowed something inarticulate and went out. I followed after her. We came down to the station as the train was pulling in. It stopped for only minutes.

"Here," I said to the stationmaster, and took his lantern and swung it over the cars. There were no marks of identification. Every car was steel, closed, strapped with bands, sometimes corrugated. There were numbers on the sides that could have meant anything: A-26804-FG, and so on. "What do you know of them?" I said to the stationmaster.

"Same as you," he said. "Only what I hear, and the less heard the better."

"Where's the conductor, the engineer?"

He pointed a thumb. "In there, having some coffee." I went to find them, but apparently they had already finished, for the train was starting up again. My wife and I stood on the platform and watched it slide away, as if it were no more than a train full of vacation-going travelers whom we had come to see off. It puffed, it chugged, it let out steam, it gathered speed exactly like any other train.

"What do you think?" I said to her as we walked home.

"I think it is the worst possible thing."

I took her arm. "We are right to fight it, aren't we?"

She was trembling. "Gustav," she said, "this is my last year of life." I bit the insides of my cheeks.

I told Kernfeffer in the morning that we had seen the train last night. We both agreed that this had become a matter of the utmost urgency, but it wasn't until April that he could bring me his friend's information. A farmer's time is in the hands of nature. I was strapped to the earth for weeks, but I did contact the several youths I knew who were most active in town, alerted all sympathizers to be ready. Again, Kernfeffer, the student Blumhauf, even two Communists brought out flyers. My admiration for these latter goes beyond words. They were working for the Committee to Rescue Asiatic Refugees and for local reform here on the school board and town council. Yet when I approached them, they did not hesitate to join me. "My God," Blumhauf said, "have we known all this since last August and still no action. Thousands of those people have passed through here by now."

"Not a single person should have passed," I said.

"Why have you been so tardy?" one of the Leninists said. The insinuation was too unjust. Words, bitterness, my dying wife choked in me. I had to walk out.

Kernfeffer ran after me. "Don't let them put a good man down," he said.

"I don't intend to," I said.

"It's their work that makes them so cranky."

I was recovering because my sense of fair play came back to me. "Still and all, they do fight, which is more than can be said for half the world, which lives in ignorance of what the other half is suffering. There," I said. We stopped by a newsstand and read the ghastly headlines that a typhoon had wiped out fifty thousand people in East

Bengal, cholera, dysentery, and starvation were expected. Refugees were fleeing everywhere.

Kernfeffer touched me on the elbow. "You should try not to read the papers if your wife is not feeling well."

His words unnerved me. I jerked my elbow away from his fingers. "My wife is perfectly well," I said, "and I shall have the largest rally this town has ever seen to halt the trains."

I went home and studied the timetable. Numbers and hours jumped in my head: Ju, My, Ju, Au, Sep, 1:05, 2:03, 4:07, FX, 2T, 8:03, Ja, Ju, Ap. My wife lay in bed, a blanket over her wasted body. God forgive me. I banged the table. The sheets, the numbers, the dates, the figures went dancing off the table. "Why wouldn't you go to a clinic," I said bitterly.

"Because there is nothing to be done," she said. "Come, sit by me and talk to me."

"I have work to do," I said crudely. I bent down and picked up the sheets and put them back in order.

"The trains?" she said.

"Yes, the trains. We are planning to have a rally, a protest they will hear in Berlin. Let me assure you, we will stop the trains."

"When?"

"When? When? When? You sound like Kernfeffer. That's what I am trying to figure out right now."

"Do it quickly."

"It cannot be done until we can all march together. What is the good if the Movement for Moral Men will not march with the Fraternity of Free Men because the Movement for Moral Men seeks to revitalize Christianity and the Fraternity of Free Men wishes to see an end to all religion. Moreover, how can I tell which of these silly little markings, A2 or BQ refers to the particular train we mean?"

"Tell them," she said, "when the train comes through you will ring the church bell as a signal, and every man, every woman, and child who loves life and would not begrudge another to live is to leave whatever he is doing and run to the station."

The simplicity of the idea was astonishing. "Excellent," I said, like Archimedes shouting Eureka. I shuffled the papers together. "No more leaping numbers, AR and FT. But how will we know in advance? We must have a lookout."

"I will watch," she said. She dragged herself up on her elbows. "Put me in that big chair there, and place me by the window. I will watch."

"But my dear, my dear, from this distance all the trains look alike."

She smiled. "Gustav," she said. She put a finger to her lips to warn me not to cry out. "I have watched death for over a year. I will not mistake it. Put the telephone by my side. When I know, I shall call the church and tell them to ring the bell, three slow tolls and a pause, and three slow tolls and a pause, and so on."

I informed the various organizations of this plan. It took me about a week to get around to the major committees. Some insisted on debating the matter. Objections were raised that only an organized pre-trained group accustomed to protest should be involved. The ordinary citizen might cause a riot or panic if he met with confrontation. The group representing Revitalized Government through Participation said they would withdraw if the whole town were not involved. Their argument was that the issue of good and evil was everybody's business, that political salvation could only come through total communal effort. A branch of the N.A.C., National Action Against Corruption, located in our town, rebutted. To them the position of the Revitalized Government through Participation was exactly that kind of murky sentiment that damns effective action, but the R.G.P. won the argument and flyers were put out all over town, letters were sent to every adult citizen. No person was left uninformed that when he heard the signal from the church he was to congregate at the railroad station and demand that the train be searched, and if the rumors be proven true, God help us, that the train be disbanded.

The Leninists said that it would be a blazing success if half the town showed up and if the half of the half that showed up protested. I asked Kernfeffer what he thought. He warned me not to be too optimistic. We walked home that night past the mine, and I could see my grandfather's figure sitting in the opening of the shaft, a lean man in a white shirt and a goatee beard blocking the passage to the dark hole by force of will. "Protest," my father said. "It is the energy of democracy." I had forgotten what heroism felt like. It had been too many years since my father had smuggled me out of Germany and I had floated down the river in the dark, making no sound of my passage. Sometimes there is only an edge between good and evil, a gesture, the gauntlet flung at the right time. If no one draws a boundary, why may not evil usurp all that there is to life. I knew that if I must, I would sit down on the track and have to take the risk of that action.

We waited for the train. Summer came. We had to renew letters, flyers, press releases. We could not let the citizenry backslide. They had to be goaded to the point and kept there. No one knew when the train would come. No doubt its schedule was part of the macabre schedule of our present state. My wife sat at the window. Every day she looked thinner. She sat by the window and knit or tried to read a book. I left her in the morning with food and tea on a tray and went out to my farm. In my mind's eye I saw the train wriggling on the horizon, floating along the track noiselessly, like a harmless toy put in motion in an atmosphere of erroneous silence, with no one to warn the town. The thought would grip me terribly at times, I would leave my work and go home, but anything that changed my routine alarmed my wife, for she gathered confidence from my assuming confidence. So I tried never to appear anxious.

Then one day, in an ordinary manner, the bells rang. I looked up from my plow and there in the distance was a black train tooting down the tracks. I got to the town in minutes, but everyone was already in the streets, dashing and running in every direction. "To the station, to the station," I yelled. The bell tolled incessantly, but everyone was dashing to cars and trucks and going in the wrong direction. Children who could hardly walk were being dragged through the streets unmercifully, old people were being bundled into cars with rough hands. I had the sickening sensation that there had been some dreadful realignment in the universe as if I had just seen a puppet come to life or waves roll backwards. I tried to stop someone, but people shook me away. "To the station," I hissed at them.

Kernfeffer caught me by the shoulder and swung me around. "The dam has broken," he said.

My knees crumpled. I whined. I bleated like a lamb.

"No, no, no. To the station I tell you."

"You only have time to save yourself," he said. My eyes were swimming with tears. People dashed past me as if I were an obstacle. And the bell kept tolling. The steeple was flattened against a perfectly blue sky. I dropped Kernfeffer's arms and ran towards my house. "Come back," he shouted after me, "it's too late even for that."

"Leone," I screamed, "my wife, my darling, my poor darling." But her intuition had ground its way into my soul, and I knew what I would find before I opened the door. She sat in the chair near the window, her forehead pressed against the glass, a doll, a puppet, a thing that had just had life, peering at the train that sped through our village.

#